Supreme Injustice

Supreme Injustice

Murdered Girl Sacrificed by the High Court

Prism Thomas

G. Stempien Publishing Company

CONTENTS

SUPREME INJUSTICE: Murdered Girl Sacrificed by the High Court

Prism Thomas

(Inside story of COX BROADCASTING CORP. ET AL v. COHN, 420 U.S. 469 (1975)

| 2 |

All court cases referred to in this work are genuine
Other works related to this topic published by G. Stempien Publishing Company:
Paris Catacombs Inscriptions: The Domain of Death by Martin Cohn
Rogue Bridge Grandmaster Martin J. Cohn by Dylan Clearfield

CONTENTS

To the Reader

TO THE READER

This is a historic fiction based on a true story. The major events described are real and only some incidentals have been fictionalized. The names of the primary characters have been changed but the roles they fill are accurately portrayed. Information about the major events has been taken from eye witnesses and direct participants.

A landmark Supreme Court decision was pronounced regarding the legal first amendment issue at the center of this story, and as of 2022 this verdict remains the prevailing law. It is a ruling that is critical to both the legal profession, journalism and the news industry, dealing with both free speech and invasion of privacy. The verdict is still studied in media law and ethics classes to this day.

I am a direct member of the victim's aggrieved family and as such have access to personal and private information that is not available to other sources. I am also a former court reporter as well as a newspaper reporter and because of this dual experience I have unique insight into the details of the courtroom activities from both the legal and news reporting perspectives.

For documentary purposes, the following is the Supreme Court case associated with this story: COX BROADCASTING CORP. ET AL v. COHN, 420 U.S. 469 (1975). Included in this fact based story are intense scenes from the original trial that led to the Supreme Court hearing. The actual - though edited - oral arguments from the Supreme Court hearing are also placed before the reader in an understandable way, showing how the final decision was reached.

What follows is a copy of the Georgia law which the Supreme Court ruled upon: "It shall be unlawful for any news media or any person to print or publish, broadcast, televise, or disseminate through any other medium of public dissemination or cause to be printed and published, broadcast, televised or disseminated in any newspaper, magazine, periodical or other publication published in this State or through any radio or television broadcast originating in the State the name or identity of any female who may have been raped or upon whom an assault with the intent to commit rape may have been made. Any person or corporation violating the provisions of this section shall, upon conviction, be punished as for a misdemeanor."

The above was the law that was broken when the victim's name in the case covered in this story was released illegally to the public by the Cable company.

1 EPSWICH, MASSACHUSETTS - JULY 18, 1971
(A true story)

Thirteen-year-old Judy Kuhn skinnied and shimmied her way out of the bedroom between her mother's bony body and the door frame as the old woman tried to block her daughter's escape. Once she'd squeezed her way free into the hallway, Judy peered back at her drunken former captor. Olga Kuhn hung from the bedroom on the door jamb in a grotesque caricature of a long-armed orangutan. The comparison was made even more pronounced by the way the swaying woman sucked in and out her thick, booze swollen lips.

She sometimes performed this puckering of the lips as an amusement for others. To complete the act, she would stretch her entire face into the shape of an ape's, thinking that this was a creative activity that required a great amount of skill not merely a natural display of her lower simian features. But Olga wasn't attempting to be entertaining now. Just cruel, hateful and vicious, traits that suited her perfectly.

Judy was a scrawny little thing for a girl her age, not overly developed in any of the places normally anticipated by a 13 year-old. Her thin physique made it easier to squeeze so agility - or maybe writhe so agility - around her mother in the doorway. One of the dubious advantages of malnutrition and a regular diet of ketchup on saltines.

Olga teetered in the doorway as Judy sped to the end of the hall and the top of the stairs. "Where do you think you're going?" drooled the slobbering drunk.

"Bike riding with Sandy. She's only got 2 days left to spend with me."

"Huh! Sandy this and Sandy that. That sister of yours is all you think about."

"That's right," Judy shouted, "she's the only good thing around here."

Sandy, who'd been listening from inside the front door, sneaked farther into the house and stationed herself at the bottom of the long flight of stairs. She was a pretty, wispy seventeen-year-old with long brunette hair and a form that had developed normally in another household where food was plentiful and not a luxury. She fearfully watched the scene taking place above.

"You little tramp!" Olga stumbled toward Judy, dragging her empty whiskey bottle behind her like the ape she personified. "You've got cleaning to do before you run off to play."

"I'll do the cleaning later."

"You'll do it now! Start with this!"

In a fit of rage, Olga flung the bottle at Judy. The girl ducked just as the projectile sailed over her head and smashed into pieces against the wall. The sound of splintering glass was like the audible shattering of the deranged woman's mind.

Olga's little black shitzu dog dodged around Sandy at the bottom of the stairs and then got the nerve to climb up to where Judy was and hysterically bark.

"Shut up, Pepper!" Judy yelled at the dog which yelped with fright then cringed back.

Guilty over her treatment of Pepper, Judy bent over the dog and petted her, apologizing.

"Leave my dog alone!" screamed Olga, staggering closer toward the top of the stairs.

"Aw, you care more for this dog than you do for me," Judy complained.

"That's right. Because she does more for me than you."

Judy started down the stairs.

"Don't you run away from me! When I get hold of you…"

No longer afraid, Pepper sprang toward Judy, tangled in her feet and knocked her down onto one of the steps. Olga grasped onto the railing and slowly crawled down it toward Judy, looking more spider like than apelike now.

"Leave her alone!" hollered Sandy from below in such a commanding voice that everyone, even the dog, froze in place. "I saw what you did, throwing that bottle at Judy. I'll tell!"

"Pah! You're as useless as your sister. Take the little tramp out of here. I've got someone coming anyway."

"I hope it's a fumigator," Sandy called over her shoulder as she and her sister rushed toward the front door.

The two girls bolted from the shadows of the old, decrepit cape cod and into the late afternoon sunshine. After navigating the rickety porch, they wended down the overgrown sidewalk toward the front gate, passing through a yard that was partially weeds, partially wild flowers, but mostly out of control grass.

"That dog of hers," Judy said.

"What about it?"

"Did I ever tell you about the time Pepper went missing and Olga went on a city-wide search for her precious dog?"

"No," replied Sandy, "I haven't heard that one yet."

"Someone called her on the phone and said they found Pepper. So I was dumped into the front seat of the old bug she used to drive and was hauled to one of the worst parts of town. She told me to duck down on the floor while she went into the apartment of the guy who said he had her dog."

"Did he have the dog or was it a trick?"

"No, he had Pepper," Judy said. "But it was a good thing it was a guy who found the dog."

"Oh, why?"

"Because he wanted a reward and Olga didn't have any money on her. But she had another way to pay."

"And I'm sure she was glad to save the money."

"More than glad," Judy replied as they pushed through the lop-sided, creaky front gate.

"She did all of this while you were scrunched down on the floor of the car!"

"Yeah. And a couple of nasty guys even looked in through the car window. I don't know how they didn't see me."

"Maybe they did," Sandy said, "and just felt sorry for you."

"More sorry than Olga ever felt for me. I stayed crunched down there for hours."

The 2 girls unhitched their bikes from the spaces between the shabby white pickets of the fence and pushed them to the dirt road.

"Let's walk until the top of the hill," Sandy suggested.

Their house was on a hillside high above town which was reached by a gently sloping but very long street.

"I can't believe dad let you stay here with her after the divorce," Sandy noted.

"I can't believe that you ever come back here to visit."

"Well it was my 17th birthday yesterday, honey, and there's no one I'd rather spend it with than you. You just happened to be living...here."

"Ha, living here? I'm more like a prisoner here."

"My stepfamily in Atlanta isn't any prize, you know. But it's sure not as bad as being here with Olga."

Both girls always referred to their mother as Olga, neither wanting to admit her parentage by calling her mother.

"But doesn't that icky step-brother of ours - Todd - keep trying to force himself on you?" asked Judy.

"Yeah, I've been able to fight him off so far. But he just doesn't stop. I don't do that stuff with him or anybody else."

"Are you telling me the real truth, sis? Not with anybody?"

"You're the one person I'd never lie to, Jude."

"You're always protecting me, Sandy." Jude was Sandy's special term of endearment for Judy, one which no one else used.

"That's what big sisters are for."

"At least if you ever need any help with your step family you have dad there to save you," observed Judy.

"Not so much. He's usually off at one bridge tournament or another. I don't see him a lot."

"I'd still rather be there than here."

"You had a choice - once."

"I was only 5 years old at the time."

"True." Sandy nodded. "You couldn't have known that your mother grew up as a Nazi and's still one."

"Nazi? Not a real one?"

"A real one. She's German and lived there till after World War 2. She was a member of the Hitler youth and was so good at it that she was selected to give the Fuhrer a bouquet of roses on one of his visits. You didn't know?"

"All I know," replied Judy, "is that she's awfully mean."

"She's more than just mean. She's a sadist. Do you know what that is?"

"A really really mean person," Judy timidly tried.

"It means that the way she treats you is criminal."

"But she is our..." she hesitated "...mother."

"And that's why you stayed behind with her?"

"She begged me to stay," said Judy. "She said if I left she would die. Just drop down dead."

"And you believed that?" Sandy asked. "That she'd just die."

"It's what she told me. What was I supposed to think?"

"Sure, she terrorized an already terrified 5-year-old. And has been terrorizing you ever since."

Sandy and Judy reached the hilltop and were just about to climb onto their bikes when a beat up old Chevy Nova chugged up beside them from the front. At the wheel was a grimy, unshaven, raggedly dressed man in his late 20's. He stopped the car, rolled down the window and asked, "Can you help me? I'm looking for 2014 Hightower Road. There's supposed to be a woman named Olga there I'm supposed to see."

"Can't be," Sandy lied to him. "I live at that address and there isn't anyone named Olga living there."

"That's crazy. Why would she give me that address then?"

"Haven't you ever been given the runaround by a woman before?"

The man in the car knowingly nodded. "Yeah, the person who told me about her did seem a little...goofy...at that. Maybe it's better that I move on."

"Maybe so," Sandy told him. "It's a bad part of town, you know."

The man started the car forward then drove to a turnabout spot in the road ahead. He turned around and drove back the way he came, waving to the 2 girls as he passed them.

"That was pretty sly," Judy said.

"You learn to think on your feet living with my step family. Looks like we won't have to worry about any unwanted male company at your place when we get back later."

"Don't be too sure of that. Olga drags them in off the street."

Sandy, however, suddenly stopped and turned a seriously frozen face toward her sister. "You don't think..." she paused, then resumed, "...you don't think that the guy we just sent away was Olga's long lost brother coming to tell her she just inherited the family fortune, do you?"

Judy was too stunned to reply.

Sandy's face abruptly burst into a smile. "I'm just kidding, Jude."

"Phew, you really scared me."

"I think a heaping helping of ice cream at the Rx will fix that," suggested Sandy. "A nice bowl of chocolate with big chippies."

"Aw, but I don't have any money."

"I just had a birthday, silly. I'm loaded. Let's go!"

The girls jumped on their bikes and whooshed down the mildly sloping road and into the small, old-fashioned town of Epswich below.

Epwich's business district was a single street of small, local shops and one stoplight. The main attraction for social gatherings was the corner drugstore - commonly known simply as the Rx - which had a lunch counter and jukebox. There was usually a group of teenagers sitting at the lunch counter and a few of them dancing to one rock song or another around the jukebox. Today, when Sandy and Judy entered the drugstore and sat at the counter they were the only ones there. But that didn't last long.

Two teenage male hotshots blew in through the front door and one planted himself beside Sandy and the other beside Judy. They weren't the delinquent types, just the nuisance types.

"Hey, whose fancy bikes are those parked out front?" The boy next to Sandy asked her.

"I guess they're ours."

"Did you ever think of putting coon tails on the ends of your handlebars?"

"Hardly ever," Sandy replied between spoonfuls of ice cream.

The boy leans far back and yanks one decorative coon tail from each front jean's pocket. He flaunts them before Sandy.

"You're in luck. I just happen to have a pair I can let you borrow."

"Borrow?"

"Sure, you test them out for a couple of days and I'll keep checking up on you to see how you like them."

Sandy shook her head. "Naw, I already don't like them. But I have a suggestion for what you can do with them."

"Would you care to demonstrate?"

"No, but I might let you know what a scoop of ice cream in your lap feels like," Sandy said

"That would be a waste of good ice cream." The boy stands up. "No sale, huh?"

"No. But I'll give you credit for a really unusual pick up line."

"Then can I possibly interest you in a high quality bike reflector?" He pulls one from his back pants pocket.

"Same terms as before?"

"Same terms."

Sandy couldn't keep from smiling. The boy was clearly harmless and even funny.

"Have a seat," Sandy offered.

"Ah, those bike reflectors are hard to resist, aren't they?" the boy joked.

"Have you told me your name yet?" Sandy asked.

"Bill. Bill Henderson. My dad owns the Epswich Bike Shop."

"I see. That's where you get your bicycle trinkets."

Bill points to the other boy. "My younger brother, Rod, works there, too. He's only 14. I'm 17."

Sandy nods toward Judy. "My younger sister, Judy."

"Wait - you must be Olga Kuhn's daughters."

"We try not to admit it," Sandy said.

"But I've never seen you before. I recognize Judy from school. Don't really see much of her outside of school."

"Her mother keeps close watch on her. I'm just visiting. Actually, I'm going to be leaving in a couple of days."

"Leaving for where?"

"Atlanta."

"That's a little far for me," said Bill.

"Right. And if any problems come up with the reflector, I'd be too far away to register any complaints."

"Okay," said Bill, standing again. "I guess I'll just mark this off as a no sale."

Sandy nods, swallowing another spoonful of ice cream.

"Maybe next time," the teen said, leaving and motioning for his brother to follow, which he did.

"What a pair," remarked Sandy.

"That happens all the time. As soon as they find out about Olga they run off like scared rabbits."

"Sometimes that's good."

"Yeah, but I never attract anybody," lamented Judy. I'm way too skinny."

"Skinny!" said Sandy. "Are you kidding? That's what boys like. You're kind of like Twiggy, that popular model."

Sandy was always trying to bolster her sister's self esteem and opinion of herself.

"Twiggy? Me?"

"Sure why not?"

Both girls had more ice cream, concentrating on the extra large chocolate chips.

"Would you have gone off with Bill?" Judy asked.

"Ha, not a chance. He doesn't seem like a bad guy, but he's still a stranger to me. I'd only get involved with someone I really know, can trust; like a classmate maybe."

"How do you know which of any of them you can trust?"

"I assume that almost every boy I meet is up to no good. They never want to just talk unless it can get them somewhere with you. I judge a boy by how his words make me feel. The sweeter the words the more sour I usually feel. Am I being used? Lied to? Made fun of? Or , sometimes, maybe even respected."

"That's not easy to learn."

"No, it isn't," Sandy replied. "But it's important."

"Yeah, some of Olga's boyfriends have a lot to say to me, figuring - like mother, like daughter. That's how that feels."

"I've got to get you out of that place. I'm going to have a real serious talk with Dad. We had no idea how bad things had gotten."

"Olga seems to have really lost her mind."

The girls became quiet at this point and concentrated on enjoying their ice cream. When they'd finished, they went outside to their bikes where a surprise awaited both of them. The ends of both of Sandy's handlebars were decorated with one coon tail each, and placed on her seat was a message from Bill weighed down by a rock. "Enjoy these at no charge."

Judy found a reflector attached to the back of her bike.. And on her seat was a note that read the same as Sandy's.

"How sweet," Sandy noted. "Seems like you have at least a couple of nice boys in this town."

The girls mounted their newly attired bikes and pedaled onward.

A couple of days later, Sandy left. A private limousine was sent by her father to pick her up and drive her to the airport for the long flight back to Atlanta. Both Judy and Olga watched her depart from behind the front gate. Olga clutched the top of Judy's bony shoulders with claw-like hands pressing firmly down upon her, keeping her in place just like she did when the little girl was first coerced into staying with the mad woman.

Sandy waved sadly goodbye through the side door window. This would be the last time Judy saw her sister alive.

2   August 17/18, 1971

Sandy sat at the dining room table with her step family in their Atlanta mansion, having returned home from Epswich a month earlier. There were 3 other people seated at the grand, glass table with Sandy, two who despised her and one who wanted to sexually maul her. In somewhat the same way that Judy was forced to hide from the atrocities of her psychotic mother and from the assaults of Olga's serial boyfriends Sandy had to evade the acidic taunts and accusations of a verbally savage and abusive step-mother, an older step-sister and to squirm from the slithery clutches of a depraved step-brother who didn't always make his advances in private. He had no shame and the others had no conscience.

Why was Sandy the object of such abuse? She was an outsider. She refused to join her step-sister Phyllis at finishing school - still an institution in 1971 among many genteel Southern households - and insisted on attending the local highschool with the common people. Sandy was an intruder from Massachusetts who came into their home - the Guilfords - as an unwanted addition from the Kuhn family after the marriage between Bette and Martin. Also Sandy could easily fit into size 6 clothing which is only something Bette and Phyllis could only dream about only after shedding 50 pounds or more.

Marty Kuhn was not at the dinner table this night - like most nights - taking part in a major bridge tournament on the West Coast. He couldn't be blamed for his frequent visits to the bridge table inasmuch as he was a grandmaster, former national champion and runner up in international competition. After selling his collection agency, Marty made most of his income from prize winnings at major bridge tournaments which he then astutely invested in the stock market, greatly expanding the initial funds.

Bette fully enjoyed those funds that were added to the amount she had already accrued from 2 previous marriages. She was devoted to acquiring possessions and needed everything she owned to "wreak" of wealth. Her marriage to Marty had been just another money-making opportunity for her. Feelings or emotion had no place in the arrangement as far as Bette was concerned. It would be easier to imagine this overweight 46 year-old matron making love to an intricately carved outrageously expensive dark green jade lampstand than with a human being. It would certainly be a perfect spiritual match.

Bette's daughter Phyliss was a smaller imitation of the mother, this being a matter where the zirconium didn't drop far from the jewelry case. So far, Phyliss's primary use for the wealth she possessed was to attract willing, pliable men.

Todd was a tall, thin 17 year-old with a long, straight nose which stuck out prominently and made up one of his main features. He was a lunk head and a reprobate and the only women who would consciously associate with him were either mentally impaired or uncommonly desperate. Todd was cruel and obnoxious and used these traits to attract women because it was the only way he could get their attention.

Bette sat at the head of the table like an overstuffed bullfrog with her meaty arms outstretched on either side of her heaping plate of food. Phyllis sat to her right and her slathering brother Todd was on the left. Sandy sat as far away from them as possible, leaving her dad's place opposite from Bette open.

Conversation at the dinner table this evening was confrontational as usual. Tonight the main subject of contention was Sandy's plan to attend the end of summer party among her classmates which was being held at one of the neighbor's estates. It was one of the neighbors whom Bette despised. But she despised most of them.

"Do you still plan to get together with those lowlife friends of yours?" Bette snapped at Sandy.

"It's better than staying here with this upstanding stepfamily."

"How dare you talk to me that way?"

"You said I was a lowlife," replied Sandy, "what do you expect?"

At this point, the two servants began looking for cover.

"Maybe I should escort you to my prep school dance next week," Todd said to Sandy.

"No, thanks."

Phyliss looked meaningfully toward her mother. "Maybe this is a good time to tell her."

"S-h-h-h." Bette hushed her. But it was too late.

"Tell me?" asked Sandy. "Tell me what!"

"Oh well," Bette sighed, " about your future, dear."

"Dear? Dear." Sandy stiffened back in her chair. "This is going to be bad, isn't it?" To be called dear by Bette was pretty much the same as being called slut.

"You're not going back to that hick filled highschool," Bette told her.

"Why not? And it's not hick filled, you're just a snob."

Bette brushed away the insult with a short cough, then said, "Your father and I decided that it would be best to send you to Mrs. Reagan's Finishing School this year."

"My father agreed to this?"

"Yes, dear," noted Bette, "he's not the complete bumpkin that he seems to be."

In fact, Martin Kuhn did not have a favorable view of women in general based on his old-fashioned upbringing. He wasn't a misogynist, but did believe that women played a subservient role in society and it was preferable that their lives be determined for them by male authority figures. He was a product of his generation. But he had not agreed to send his daughter to a finishing school.

"So you see," Phyliss told Sandy, "there's no need for you to attend this grimy school party."

"Not even to say goodbye to my friends?"

"They'll be history soon," said Todd.

"Well, I'm still going to the party." Sandy slowly pushed away from the table. "Carly's going to be here in a half hour to pick me up. I need to get ready."

Todd waited at the table for a couple of minutes before he got up to follow Sandy to her room. He calculated just the right time to arrive there which would find his step-sister in a partial state of undressing. His calculations proved accurate as Sandy was caught in bra and bell bottom jeans when Todd lunged unannounced through her door. Sandy immediately retreated to the bathroom.

She couldn't lock the door because the lock was broken, a piece of vandalism performed by Todd when he realized Sandy wouldn't be easy to trap.

"Getting ready for tonight?" Todd laughed, dropping into the chair before Sandy's dressing table. "Dressing down I see."

"Will you get out of here!" Sandy's voice was amplified by the echo given to it by the bathroom's acoustics.

"I just got here."

"Then just get out again!"

"You better be nice to me," said Todd.

"I am being nice. I'm not screaming my head off."

"Who'd hear you?"

"Anyone in the house."

"You know they won't bother," noted Todd.

"The neighbors might bother."

"Too far away in their big mansions to hear you."

"I'll report you to the police."

"They won't believe you."

"You've figured this all out, haven't you?"

"I've planned a lot."

"What do you want anyway?"

"What every man wants."

"From his own sister?"

"Step-sister."

"Just a word - not a real sister."

"Real enough for me," Sandy replied. "Unfortunately, it implies some form of relationship between us."

Todd peered over his shoulder at the portrait of Judy that hung on the wall to the upper right of the dressing table mirror.

"You must think a lot about your little sister to keep a picture of her on the wall."

Sandy didn't respond.

"She's cute. Skinny."

"She's 13."

"But she has promise."

"Not for you she doesn't."

"Hey, what would I have to do to get my picture on your wall?" Todd slimed.

"Do you really want to know?"

"Come on, don't be like that. You know how you really feel about me."

"I'm trying to keep it under control."

"Can't keep your hands off me, huh?"

"Yeah, from right around your miserable throat."

Todd gets up from the chair. "I'm getting tired of all this chit chat. Hey, how about we take a quick shower together?"

The thought sickened Sandy to the point that she had to control a choking reaction in her throat. Todd was stalking toward the bathroom; Sandy had to think quickly. An idea came.

"We can't take a shower until I clear the spider out of the bathtub."

Todd froze in place. "The...what?"

"Spider. You know, those nastly little things with eight long legs and that like to bite people."

Todd suffered from an unnatural, phobic fear of spiders - any kind of spider. Sandy knew this. Todd's spider terror began when he was an infant. One day he was trapped in his crib when a group of spiders paid him a visit. He squealed in horror and cringed in the corner of the crib. Ignoring his wails, it took several minutes for the governess to finally come to his aid but by that time Todd had acquired his dread of spiders. Sandy now put knowledge of this to good use.

"I caught him in one of my empty shampoo bottles," she called out to Todd. "Want to see him? He's very friendly. He'll probably want to crawl all over you."

Sandy peeked into the bedroom. It was vacant; Todd had fled. Not knowing when he'd return - only that he would - Sandy quickly finished dressing, took up her pocketbook, then scurried toward the front door.

She sprinted the short distance to where her friend Carly was waiting behind the wheel of a green VW rabbit. Carly was a hippie type 17 year-old with long, straight black tresses and whose favorite attire was tunic shirts and wide bell bottoms. She smoked lots of weed and was Sandy's best friend.

"Wow, who's chasing you?" asked Carly.

"Who do you think?" said Sandy, adjusting herself in the passenger seat.

"From your house - could be anybody. But probably Todd."

"Right the first time," replied Sandy as the car jerked forward and started down the long, shrub-lined semi-circular driveway. "He had me pretty well cornered tonight. I should've expected it, but my mind was on something else."

"What?"

"Mrs. Reagan's Finishing School. They want to send me there."

"Congratulations!" cried Carly

"What? Congratulations?"

"Sure, you got to them and totally freaked them out."

"It might be a moral victory - I guess - but I don't know what I'm going to do."

"You could come and live with me."

"Naw, they'd just haul me back and then maybe deport me to Massachusetts to serve out my sentence under my lunatic mother."

They drove on aways before Sandy acknowledged, "Wow, after everything that happened to me today, I could really use a drink...or a few."

"Take it easy, kid," warned her friend, "I know you and you're no drinker."

"Tonight I'm going to be one."

The car turned off the main road and onto the long, climbing driveway that led to the Reynolds Mansion on the hill, the site of the wild party. The house was of a sprawling ranch style design hidden in a wooded 5 acre estate. It was the ultimate in privacy. Even better, Mr. and Mrs. Reynolds were enjoying a trip to Africa and the property was under the control of their teenage sons, Bob and Frank.

Carly pulled her car into the parking area that fronted the 4 bay wide garage. It was relatively quiet here because all of the activity was out back near the pool/tennis court. The two girls left the car and entered under the collonaded walkway that led to where the party was. The music of "Fire and Rain" by James Taylor wafted over them, echoing from the sophisticated sound system that supplied the popular tunes of the day to the rolicking guests. Sandy wasted no time merging into the horde of gyrating, heavy drinking, drug-using teens as Carly sought out her particular clique to announce her own arrival.

When Carly looked for Sandy again later, she found her friend to be in a state of greatly diminished capacity - she was drunk - and who'd become the unwitting plaything for a group of just as inebri-ated boys. They were all her age, none younger than 17 or older than 18; and all of them were classmates of hers.

"Sandy, I never saw you this way before," said Carly, taking a bottle of whiskey from her hand.

"And I...I never *swah* you this...this way before *eeffer*," her friend slurred and mispronounced words. "You're kinda blurry."

Carly read the contents of the bottle more closely, then noted, "These guys are trying to get you drunk. This brand has twice the alcohol content than others like it."

"Who...who's counting? Are you my mother or something? If you...are, I *reamy feeble* sorry for you."

"No, I'm your friend."

"Well, these are my friends, too," replied Sandy, making a sweeping gesture over the group of 6 boys who'd circled around her. "And they're going to drive me home instead of you. They said I could trust them to get me there safe and sound."

"And we're leaving right now," One of the boys, namedChad, told Carly.

"I hope one of you is sober enough to drive."

"Oh, that would be Kevin," Chad laughed. "He's the teetotaler of the group."

With that, the group of 6 classmates staggered - except for Kevin - away from the pool area and down the collonaded walkway toward the parked cars. The original intention of the boys wasn't to harm Sandy but to seduce whatever favors they could from her as those of their gender are known to do. Sandy was unawares. Not because she was naive but because her common sense had been strongly diluted by the effects of the alcoholic content of her drink.

The group stumbled on toward a spacious, late model Lincoln Continental and it was decided that Sandy would ride in the back somewhere between Tyler, Sean, and Eric. Tyler and Sean got in first and as Sandy started her climb into the car she lost consciousness and was lifted over the others like a limp flannel doll and was placed across their laps. The other 3 boys piled into the front seat.

"Great! She's passed out; now what do we do with her?" asked Tyler as Kevin started the car forward.

"Here's your chance to lose your virginity, Ty," Chad suggested.

"But she's unconscious," Replied Tyler.

"The best chance you'll ever get," Bill laughed from the front seat.

"Go for it!" urged Chad.

"Yeah, you go first and then we'll take turns with her," Eric said.

"Good idea," responded Chad. "Let's find a place to pull over. We can't do this in a moving car."

"Right," answered Kevin. "I think there's a pull off place just ahead off the main road."

A secluded spot was located off the side of the road and one by one 5 of the 6 boys had their way with Sandy, far worse than the common way that boys take "favors" from the other gender. Tyler refused to participate, preferring to lose his virginity in a situation where the other person was also participating in the event.

Last to assault Sandy was Sean. But he alone recognized that she was not simply unconscious. When he emerged from the car, he said with a hollow, terrified voice, "Hey guys, I think she's dead."

Acting as one, each of them leapt toward the car to peer into the back at their motionless victim. Sandy lay in a contorted position, unmoving. The boys reeled backward from the scene and discussed the new situation.

"Now what do we do?" asked Kevin.

"Get rid of her," said Chad. "Dump her somewhere."

"But she's our...friend," Tyler, the only one who hadn't participated in the girl's molestation, reminded him.

"Not anymore - she's dead," replied Chad.

"We have to get rid of the body!" urged Sean. "They'll think we killed her."

"Didn't we!" asked Bill.

"I don't know," said Chad. "How did we kill her? None of us hit her or roughed her up."

"No, we just raped her," said Eric.

"Just! Just raped her?" Tyler repeated, incredulous.

"How could that actually kill anyone, though?" Sean asked.

"It doesn't matter," Chad replied. "She died while with us. We'll get blamed."

Kevin started crying. "I didn't want this to happen."

"Shut up," said Chad. "None of us did. It was an accident and we have to think about ourselves now."

"So what do we do?" Bill asked.

"Drive to a neighbor's house and get some help."

"Help for a dead person?" Bill responded.

"Are we sure she's really dead?" asked Kevin. "Huh? Are we?"

"Okay! Okay," barked Chad, "we'll pull into the first driveway we come to and ask for help."

The boys all got back into the car and Chad drove on, a thick silence burying all of their thoughts. After a couple of minutes a house appeared ahead on the right.

Chad turned into the driveway that led to another of the local mansions. Kevin leapt out of the car and ran to the front door. It was late and the house was dark, but he kept rapping until someone answered. An elderly, slumped over man wearing a smoking jacket yanked open the door and asked with great annoyance, "What do you want at this hour?"

"We have a friend who needs help," cried Kevin. "She's in the car and we don't know…"

Mr. Jones, whose home this was, cut him off. "You're drunk! I can smell it on your breath. Get out of here or I'll call the police."

"No, listen…"

Mr. Jones didn't listen and slammed the door in Kevin's face. Kevin returned to the car.

"Well?" asked Sean.

"He thought I was drunk and threatened to call the police."

"What now!" squawked Bill.

"Take her back to her house like we planned," replied Chad.

"What!" squealed Kevin. "And just carry her dead body inside?"

"No, leave it outside by the front door," Chad told him. "It'll look like someone brought her home and she died at the front door."

"Just died! For no reason? Tyler questioned.

"The booze killed her," Chad answered. "Everybody saw how much she was drinking tonight. Even Carly will swear to that."

"And how do we explain what physically happened to her?" Sean asked. "It's obvious she was...uh... manhandled."

"We don't try to explain it," Chad said. "Just say it must've happened during the party sometime."

"Hey, that's good," Eric agreed. "No one can prove we did anything to her."

"Yeah, except the 6 of us," noted Sean.

"Okay then, that's the plan," Chad finalized. "We just drive her home."

The boys got back into the car. They drove to Sandy's home, stealthily crawled up the long driveway and parked not far from the dark house's front door, but not in too close sight either. Eric and Chad hoisted Sandy's body from the car and dragged her between them to the front door. They laid the dead body on the doorstep, rang the bell and ran off as if playing a Hallowe'en prank.

3

Martin Kuhn - also known simply as Pitt - was an imposing man both physically and verbally. When the broad shouldered, bespectacled, 6' 2," 45 year-old entered a room it tilted toward him - all attention sliding in his direction. Although often intimidating, he was never a bully. He was well known among the fairer sex and his powerful voice could make a lady quiver or quake, depending on the situation. In a romantic setting, a woman's heart would quiver with excitement and expectation; in a less friendly environment she might quake at the threat of being issued a verbally firm correction. But Marty was never cruel and always maintained a standard of dignity and decency.

On this fateful night he was attending a bridge tournament in San Francisco with his friend, personal attorney and card partner, Bob Larson. Bob was in most ways unlike Marty - somewhat shorter, slender of build, quiet of voice and not what would be termed a "ladies man." They were opposites of personality and as such were never in direct competition which allowed for a successful working relationship both at the bridge table and when attending to legal matters. This compatible working relationship was going to be critical for Marty, considering the tragic news he was about to receive.

Marty had just made one of his patented shocking bridge plays which won the rubber.

Larson fell back in his seat, noting, "A natural over Kuhn, 3-1 fit victory. I'm glad you made all the play in advance and kept me in the dark - as usual."

"I couldn't let you in on the strategy. You might've sabotaged it without knowing."

"That's why we work so well together. You make the calls and I don't interfere."

They were interrupted by a stern-faced tournament official, carrying a silver tray with a telegram on it. "For you, Mr. Kuhn," he said, laying the tray on the table beside him. He then stepped back and waited in case there was a reply.

Marty took a drink from his snifter of cognac, a tug on his thick, ever present Havana cigar, then picked up the envelope and began to slowly tear it open at one end.

Larson noted, "Telegrams are never good news."

"Right, good news waits to be announced," replied Marty, drawing in on his havana, "while bad news always demands attention."

Marty adjusted the horn rimmed glasses on the bridge of his nose and then slid the soft textured paper from its cocoon. He read the grim note, then fell back in his seat with a puff of smoke, shaking his head.

"How bad is it?"

Marty cleared his throat. "My...my daughter, Sandy. She was found dead about 3 hours ago."

"What! My God!"

"That's all the telegram says." Marty's eyes darted in confusion around the tabletop, processing how to mourn for a daughter he seldom saw but nonetheless loved with all his heart.

Larson reached for the note and Marty vacantly handed it to him. He then nodded to the waiting attendant, dismissing him.

"I've got to get out of here," said Marty, standing with difficulty, caused by the sudden emotional jolt.

Larson also got up.

Marty addressed the surprised bridge players at their table. "There's been an emergency. We have to leave right away. We concede the rest of the match."

He and Larson started across the room.

Others were also being given the news of Sandy's sudden death. In Epswich, her mother Olga received an early morning phone call from the local police, a call which she answered only because the phone was in the kitchen where she was heading to get another beer from the refrigerator. Olga was barely sober enough to be able to hold the receiver to her ear and tottered by the wall phone. An anxious Judy, who'd been asleep in a kitchen chair, got up and stood next to her mother, trying to make sense of the conversation while at the same time keeping the excited dog in control.

"What?" Olga slurred into the phone. "What...what about Sandy?"

Judy pressed closer, distressed.

"Found her where?" Olga asked the caller. "Doorstep? What...doorstep?"

"Is she all right?" Judy asked her mother who ignored her. "Is she all right?"

"What happened to her?" Olga stammered into the phone.

There was silence, except for the dog's continued whining.

"She's dead?" Olga blurted. "Dead? How?"

Judy dropped to the floor in shocked grief and almost fell on the dog who ran off yelping in fright.

"You...you don't know yet?" Olga asked. "Okay. You'll let me know when you...when you have more information."

That ended the conversation and Olga hung up the phone.

"Well, you probably heard, your sister's dead," Olga casually told Judy, then finished her trip to the nearby refrigerator.

"But what happened?"

"They don't know yet," said Olga, opening the refrigerator door and yanking out a beer. "Now I'll have to haul you down to Atlanta for the funeral."

"Don't you even care about Sandy?" Judy demanded.

"Sure, I care. But it would've been better if you were the one who was dead instead of her."

How does a 13 year-old respond to such a cruel and hateful statement from her own mother? First, there's stunned shock. Then there's the need to flee. That's what Judy did, rushing outside onto the front porch where she fell into the swing and started to cry. Olga followed her to the door and locked it behind her, muttering to herself, "Yep, would've been a lot better if she'd been the one who'd died tonight."

A third person was also at that time learning of Sandy's sudden death - her best friend, Carly. After being summoned to the Kuhn home upon discovery of Sandy's body, the police dispatched a squad to the location of the wild teen party at the Reynolds estate. There were still participants on hand, and Carly was the primary person that the investigating sergeant questioned. That's when the identities of the 6 boys who gave Sandy a ride home were revealed to authorities. They too were questioned, but all of them at police headquarters.

The 6 boys were arrested and booked on charges ranging from attempted rape to the actual rape of a juvenile female and her murder. The murder charge was eventually dropped because the coroner had determined in his preliminary exam that death had been the result of alcoholic poisoning with the victim ultimately dying by choking on her own vomit and the time of death could not with certainty be placed at the moment the rapes were occurring.

The 6 were quickly released on bail, all of them belonging to affluent well connected families in the Atlanta area. A plea deal was quickly fashioned by the defense and the district attorney and was to be presented to Martin Kuhn and his attorney. The families of the accused wanted to get this over with and covered up...quickly!

4

Olga and Judy drove in the family car to Atlanta to attend Sandy's funeral. It was arranged that when Olga returned to Epswich that Judy would remain behind and stay with her dad and step family.

She was given her sister's old bedroom which was still filled with Sandy's things.

Judy's first evening spent with her new family was excruciating. It began at the dinner table - the day of the funeral - with the wrathful trio seated in their usual positions, picking at the defenseless girl with the eyes of vultures. Judy randomly seated herself at her sister's former place, perhaps drawn to it by a magnetic spiritual attraction.

"Too bad your dad couldn't be here," smirked Bette from the head of the table where she sat draped with jewelry.

"We know what that's about," accused Phyllis, "he's too busy meeting with the district attorney tonight because he just couldn't wait to protect himself."

"He's there to protect Sandy's name," Judy spoke out.

"Sure," replied Phyllis, "so he doesn't look so bad as a father."

"Wait a minute now," Todd entered the fray, pretending to help Judy. "Let's be fair. Marty's only doing what he thinks is right."

"Shut up you worm!" snapped Phyllis. "All you want is to make points with your new little sister."

"I'd trade her for you any day," said Todd.

"Nobody ever accused you of having any taste," responded Phyliss with a sneer.

"Nobody trades me for anything!" spoke out Judy.

"Speaking of trading places," said Bette, "it sure looks like that instead of sending Sandy back to her mother, like we'd hoped to do, that drunk Olga dumped another daughter on us."

"This house belongs to my dad, you know." returned Judy. "Did you forget that?"

"Too bad he's so seldom here," replied Bette.

Judy fought back. "Maybe it's because of the type of people who live here. He can't stand to be around them!"

"And the feeling's mutual!" shot back Bette.

The two servants came to the table and removed some of the dishes, glasses and particularly the knives.

Bette resumed speaking to Judy, "Since you were dropped off on us with such short notice we haven't had any time to make any changes to your sister's old room which is where we're placing you."

"I still think Judy should've been given a smaller, less fancy room," snapped Phyllis, "and you should let me take over Sandy's old one for some of my art projects."

Todd laughed, "Art projects you call them. Junk by any other name."

"Yeah, and you're a bastard by all other names!" Phyllis yowled at her brother.

Bette pounded the tabletop with both meaty fists. "Enough! Dinner is over." She nodded toward Phyllis, "Show Judy to her room."

With great reluctance, the overweight young woman hoisted herself up and motioned to Judy to follow her.

"If you need any help..." cawed Todd.

"Help yourself another time," his sister told him. She then led Judy down a long hallway to a room at its end. On the door was taped the picture of two horses, touching snouts in friendship.

"This must be Sandy's room," Judy said as they stood outside the door. "She really liked horses."

"Maybe that's why her room was like a stable."

Judy peered at Phyllis. "Why do you hate us so much?"

"Why? Because you're outsiders, intruders. You don't belong here. But you take over the place like you own it."

"Why do you even hate Todd?" asked Judy.

Phyllis smirked. "He even tried to hit on me. He's sick, really. Insane. But that doesn't excuse him."

"Is he dangerous?" questioned Judy.

Phyllis turned to leave, saying as she did, "I...I'm not really sure. I guess you'll find out."

Phyllis departed. Judy opened the door to her sister's room. It was anything but a stable. It was the neat, proper room of a decent young lady. Judy slowly passed through the room, touching objects where they lay - Sandy's sling purse hanging on the back of a chair, a hairband on the dressing table next to a brush and an array of cosmetics lined up like a feminine version of toy soldiers to take part in the dating battles of the sexes.

But what she saw next made her freeze in place. Judy threw her hands to her face and began to cry. Streaming from either side of the air conditioning vent in the ceiling above the bed were the 2 coon tails given to Sandy as a present by the boy in the Epswich drug store. She hadn't any idea what a deep impression that memory had made on her.

Later Sandy would be accused of using poor judgment - and even worse - in accepting a ride home from the 6 boys who ended up killing her. But she wasn't a foolish girl; she'd learned well how to judge the motives of those of the opposite sex as demonstrated in her assessment of the boys at the drugstore on that special evening with her sister. On the night of the teen party at the Reynold's estate Sandy knew she needed help getting home and sought it from who should've been 6 trustworthy classmates.

Judy continued visiting the room and its contents. At first she was uneasy being surrounded by her sister's many personal possessions. But then she began to take comfort from them, even trying on some of her clothing, including one of Sandy's bras which Judy was shocked to find almost fit her. Trying on her sister's clothes wasn't that unusual since they used to exchange all kinds of pieces of clothing when...when Sandy was still alive. Now dressing up like Sandy made Judy feel closer to a sister no longer here.

Judy unfit the bra and placed it into a drawer. She re-buttoned her blouse and straightened out the rest of her clothes. Judy then snatched Sandy's purse from the chair and, hugging it to her breast, shuffled to the bed and dropped into it, sobbing.

5

Marty Kuhn couldn't be there for his besieged daughter Judy because he was attending the conference to deal with the legalities concerning the murder of his other daughter. A very grim group was gathered in the Fulton County district attorney's opulently furnished office for this special mid evening meeting. The subject was the death of one innocent girl, the crimes of her 6 attackers and the plea deal that had been so rapidly designed.

Seated behind the great desk was the District Attorney Ryan Kliner. To his right was the official court reporter. Assembled in a small group before the desk was Jackson Frembry, lead defense attorney for the accused boys, Bob Larson the attorney for the victim's family, and Marty Kuhn, an imposing sentinel at the end of the short row of men. Except for Marty, Larson, and the female court reporter, the others in the room looked like well dressed mannequins of little imagination - a couple of them wearing glasses. The rest of the spacious room was unoccupied.

Marty was working on his ever present havana and would've also been sipping on a snifter of cognac if not dissuaded from bringing it into the meeting by his lawyer. It wasn't that Marty disrespected the process, just that he gave preference to his usual unchecked habits. Few people challenged his right.

"Thank you all for coming on such short notice. I am Fulton County District Attorney, Ryan Kliner."

"Thank you for expediting the case," said Fremby. "It deserves immediate attention. The boys' families are terribly anxious."

"Yes, and the public has become overly interested in this matter and it's best to dispose of it as quickly as possible."

"Dispose of?" grunted Marty. "That makes it sound like something you are trying to get rid of rather than adjudicate properly."

"You're quite right," replied Kliner, "it was a poor choice of words. However, this case is in the forefront of public interest and must be arbitrated in a timely manner."

"Let's get on with it," said Jackson Fremby, the man seated next to Larson on the opposite side of Marty.

"First, for official purposes, I'll identify those present," Kliner went on. The man who just spoke is Jackson Fremby the defense attorney representing the 6 accused. Martin Kuhn, the victim's father, is also here and is accompanied by his attorney, Robert Larson. I have already introduced myself and I am prosecuting this case for the state. A court reporter is on hand to keep a legal record of this meeting."

He didn't need to share the information that the father of one of the defendants was a well-placed attorney who had been instrumental in establishing the Kerner Cable Corporation that had aired the telecast revealing Sandy's identity to the public. Or that another parent of one of the accused was a very well known surgeon. Wealth had a great deal to do with the final outcome of this case and everyone knew it.

A silent moment passed, then Kliner resumed. "The case has been thoroughly investigated. All evidence has been secured, all witness testimony has been gathered and the events of the night of August 17th and 18th are clear. The official findings are that Sandy Kuhn was driven to a secluded spot in the company of the 6 defendants where she was raped and was later driven in the company of the same 6 to the place where she lived and was there left in an unconscious state on the doorstep after which the culprits drove away without reporting the incident."

"A deceased condition," said Larson. "So we were summoned together tonight to consider a plea deal by the defense?"

"Yes," continued Kliner. "The defense has agreed to plead guilty to the charges of rape and attempted rape in exchange for dropping the murder charges."

"Why would we accept that?" Marty asked.

"If the state accepts the plea deal," Kliner explained, "that would avoid the necessity of holding a formal trial. Your attorney advised us that you wanted as little publicity as possible. That it was very important to you. This is the best way to avoid publicity"

"But my daughter was murdered."

"Actually," said Fremby for the defense, "the coroner has not been able to determine that as a fact."

"She is dead, and she died while in the hands of those...killers," said Marty.

"That she is dead is beyond dispute," replied Kliner, "but not necessarily murdered. What is uncertain is the precise time of death which is of critical importance."

"And the official stated cause of death is alcohol poisoning," Fremby added.

"She was killed," Marty said.

"Yes, but as the result of choking on her own vomit not necessarily from the treatment of the attackers," replied Kliner.

"Even so," argued Marty, "they were still the cause of her death. It's been reported by witnesses that they gave her the alcohol which you say also could have contributed to her death."

"That's true, Marty," broke in Larson, his attorney, "but there isn't any way to prove that her attackers were the actual cause of her drinking enough of the alcohol so as to lead to the point of death."

"So they get off with a lesser charge and a slap on the wrist."

"We avoid a formal trial and get a guaranteed sentencing," Larson noted. He then turned toward Fremby, "What type of sentencing is the defense expecting?"

"All 6 defendants to plead guilty to charges of rape or attempted rape and to receive sentences ranging from 5 years for rape to 2 years for the attempted rape."

"Only 2 years!" cried Marty.

"That's a pretty lenient plea deal," Larson complained.

"Remember," Kliner responded, "it would circumvent a trial which would keep the victim's name from being made public. And it would be extremely difficult anyway to prove a charge of murder based on the evidence."

"But only 5 years at the worst!" Marty shook his head.

"The affair would be kept from becoming a news spectacle on television," Fremby responded.

"The price for privacy might be too high," said Larson.

"But to see my daughter's good name splashed all over television..." Marty groaned.

"I feel obliged to tell you, Mr. Kuhn," Kliner the D.A. spoke, "getting a murder conviction would be very difficult and, I think, pretty much out of the question. And, if this were to go to trial, the defense would do everything possible to make your daughter the guilty party and destroy her reputation as best they could."

"Yes, I see."

"In all honesty," Larson told Marty, "I'd spend most of my time defending Sandy. They'd claim that she lured the boys out to the secluded spot and then..."

Marty interrupted him, waving a hand up and down. "Yes, yes, I know. I've seen how it's done in the tabloids."

"So, you see, Mr. Kuhn," Kliner said, "accepting the plea bargain is the best option."

Marty removed his glasses, braced forward in his seat and fastened his eyes onto Kliner's. Their stares locked. The room shivered, then froze. Marty asked the D.A. "Can you assure me that if we accept this plea deal that my daughter's name will never be made public?"

"Yes, I can."

"How can you be so certain?"

"It is a criminal violation in this state to make public the name of a juvenile rape victim. Your daughter was a juvenile."

"A criminal violation?"

"So ruled by the Supreme Court of Georgia. If you agree to the plea deal it would be a criminal offense for anyone to publicly reveal your daughter's name."

"Do you guarantee that?" Marty pressed.

"I guarantee it."

Marty repositioned the glasses on his nose, purposefully sat back in his chair and turned his head toward Larson, silently peering at him. The room creaked.

"Then I agree," said Marty.

Kliner sat back as well. "Very good. Then we'll draw up the official documents for your signatures and present them to Judge Wilson for his approval. Does everyone here officially agree?"

"Yes," said Frembly.

"I agree," Larson spoke out.

Marty simply nodded. But when urged by the court reporter, said a weak, "Me, too."

It was important to get verbal agreement from all the primary participants so the court reporter could record them.

"Very well, then this concludes the meeting. You will be hearing from this office within the week."

Chairs shuffled and scraped the floor as everyone prepared to leave. Larson said to Marty, "Well, it looks like it's just about all over."

Marty slowly shook his head and replied, "No, somehow I think this is only the beginning."

6

A large gathering of protesters had assembled on the rolling lawn of the local highschool the evening after the meeting with the district attorney had taken place. These people were angry. The protest was attended mostly by highschool students but there was also a representative appearance made by the general population of the area. What they wanted was the release from custody of the group of teenage boys which had become known as the Sandy Springs 6.

A small stage had been set up constructed of sections of fitted aluminum that were used to build stands for sporting events. Three self-appointed spokespersons - highschool boys from the local school - took turns alternately clomping up and down the stage, shouting slogans and shaking their fists. The primary chant was: "Free the Sandy Springs 6" accompanied by, "Reveal their accuser" which meant the girl they had victimized. And, "She's a slut!!"

Also attending this protest was the local cable television on-the-spot news crew, led by 23 year-old Allan Morton. Mr. Morton had been an on-the-scene reporter for about 5 years and was desperate to advance from this background position to an anchor spot. He was ruthless and persistent and had little concern for the feelings or the rights of others. Mr. Morton believed that if he could extract by any means the name of the victim in this widely followed case and reveal it on live television he would be thrust to the top of the newsroom promotions list.

After the rally had worn itself out and was dispersing, Morton called the main ringleader over to the edge of the stage, an 18 year-old pampered rich boy and big mouth, Cull Winslow.

"Can I have your name for the viewing audience?" Morton asked.

"Cull. Cull Winslow."

"Do you go to school here at Sandy Springs High, Cull?"

"Sure do. I'm a senior."

"What's the message you want to get out to the people of Sandy Springs? We're live on the air now."

"That my 6 classmates are being unfairly treated. They took a girl for a ride home from a party and she died on the way. Is that their fault?"

"There is also a charge of rape and aggravated battery against them," Morton noted.

"Maybe she shouldn't have been with them in the first place," he spat.

"Then you're claiming she is to blame for her own attack?"

"Nobody forced her to get into that car with 6 boys. She knew what she was getting into."

"But the 6 did plead guilty to the lesser charges."

"They were railroaded. They didn't have a choice. Just because a girl accuses them they're automatically guilty. And who is she anyway? Why won't they tell us who this slut is?"

"From what I've heard, the authorities won't release her name because she's a minor."

"I guess that's as good an excuse as any," Cull said.

"So you want her name to be released?"

"Sure I do! After all, what harm could it do?"

With that, Morton turned away from the stage and addressed the viewing audience. "The leader of the protest asked: what harm could it do to release the victim's name? Many people agree with his sentiments as noted by the response of the crowd here tonight. For Cable 7 News, this is Allan Morton from the protest outside Sandy Springs Highschool. Good night."

The newscast wrapped up. As Morton and the others tended to packing their gear, one of the bystanders at the protest approached the head of the news crew. It was Bob Larson.

"Interesting report," Larson told him.

"You look familiar? Do I know you?"

"You've probably seen me on television," Larson said with a glint. "I'm representing the murdered girl."

"Murdered? I thought it was rape."

"Well, our theory is that the multiple rapes are what caused her death."

"But you can't prove that?" replied Morton.

"I can't discuss that."

"What brings you out here tonight?" Morton asked.

"Just curious as to the type of crowd such a rally would raise. I see that the concept of Sandy Springs being a Golden Ghetto where the rich can make their own laws and get away with murder is factual."

"Oh, I thought you might've dropped by to reveal the victim's name."

"Why do you so desperately want her identity?"

"Not me, Mr. Larson, it's the people who want to know who she is."

"Could it be because you put that idea into their heads?"

Laughingly, "You give me credit for too large of a viewership."

"Maybe so, maybe so." Larson nodded. "But it seems that this story is one way to grow your viewership."

"What's wrong with that? It's a big story. A big chance for me."

"I overheard a little of your talk with that...rabble rouser high-school kid," Larson told him. "Do you think your reporting is fair and unbiased?"

"I report it like I see it."

"Or how the rabble rousers see it. You're only telling one side of the story. What about the victim?"

"What does it matter to her - she's dead?"

"It matters to her family and those who knew and loved her. Who's speaking for her?"

"Why - you are Mr. Larson. You're her attorney."

"I'd like to tell your audience a few things. That there wasn't anything inappropriate in the victim's behavior like you and the others implied. For one thing, she asked fellow classmates for a ride home, not a group of strange and unknown men. Or is there some reason that a girl shouldn't ask for help?"

"Maybe if she hadn't fallen down drunk..."

"But it's okay if any of the boys get so drunk they take a girl for a ride that ends in her death."

"It happened like it happened."

"I guess the ratings must be better when attacking a girl rather than defending her."

"Look, I don't make public sentiment, Mr. Larson, I just report on it."

"Are you sure?" Larson turned to leave, but then added, "I hope you end up with what you expect and not what you don't."

"What's that supposed to mean?"

"Are you prepared to suffer for your cause?" Larson asked.

"Stop with the lawyer talk. Say what you mean to say."

"Well. you're so anxious to divulge the name of the victim - did you know that it's a crime in this state to reveal the identity of a juvenile female rape victim?"

Morton was caught off guard. "I...I wasn't sure."

"You might want to examine the law on this matter before blurting out the name of an innocent victim all over the air."

Larson started on his way, leaving a bewildered on-the-scene reporter in his wake.

7

The old-fashioned courtroom was furnished with rows of wooden pew like benches. The wide, dark room had the aroma of hardwood and a sense of gravity left by past judicial proceedings that hung like a mist in the subdued light. At the front of the chamber loomed the judge's high bench, a massive, wooden monolith demonstrating the power and weight of the law. Not necessarily justice. It was beneath this law that so many women had been disproportionately crushed over the years.

Cringing at the foot of the judge's bench near its center was a long, but narrow desk which was already occupied - the clerk on one end and the court reporter on the other. Facing the judge's bench were the tables used by the defense and the prosecution, separated by the main central aisle. Lined up behind the tables were the appropriate number of chairs that had been set up for this hearing.

Marty and Larson had arrived early and were waiting in one of the front row pews. There was a corps of news reporters on hand who fiddled with their notepads, pencils, microphones and tape recorders at various locations, awaiting the main event. Among them was Allan Morton, on-the-scene t.v. reporter.

Assorted family members of those who were about to be sentenced sat in a group mostly huddled together in the center of the courtroom, presenting a collection of mink coats, gaudy jewelry and 3 piece suits. After all, Sandy Springs was a wealthy bedroom community even though its children might have been juvenile delinquents.

The solemn atmosphere was bruised by the sound of some of the participants in the upcoming hearing entering through a side door. A defendant's mother screamed in shock. It was the 6 defendants being escorted into the chamber by armed guards. They wore jumpsuits and were in ankle chains which made quite a din, clinking and clanking together and scraping the floor. Their lawyer and his various legal assistants followed them. As one, the defendants were aligned before the chairs behind the defendant's desk and ordered to sit; they took their seats in a tumult of noise that sounded louder than it should.

A couple of the reporters rushed toward the defendants to sneak interviews, but were prevented from doing so by the armed guards. Their attorney, Frembly, attempted to speak to one of the reporters but he too was held off by the guards.

"Sorry," Fremby cried out to the reporters, "you can see how the defense is being treated."

There was a loud bang at the back of the room as the bailiff slammed the door shut and locked it from the inside, remaining there on guard. The pictures that lined the walls of the old men who'd served this court in the past trembled from the vibration.

"Because this case involves juveniles," Larson told Marty, "it isn't open to the public."

"But it is to the press?"

"They usually get their way."

"But not always their interview," noted Marty.

"They won't give up, though. There's a great deal of interest in this case. They've got a television crew set up on the courthouse steps to give live results."

"The last thing I want - publicity."

"It could've been worse, old friend."

A moment later, the district attorney Kliner entered through a side door with his two assistants, bearing armfuls of legal documents. Kliner proceeded to the prosecution's table and was joined there by Marty and Larson. After a brief exchange of pleasantries they took their seats next to one another at the table while the assistants were already settled behind them in one of the benches.

"This shouldn't take long," Kliner spoke. "All of the preliminaries have already been hammered out."

The judge then entered through the door that was behind the bench. He was a tall, balding man in his late fifties with a long, emotionless face. Everyone arose at his entrance, and remained standing since that was required for this type of proceeding. Step by step the process of the law unfolded, following its usual ritualistic procedures.

The judge surveyed his domain from the legal throne. "Are all of the principals in attendance?" he queried.

"Yes, your honor," replied Kliner, Larson and Fremby in unison.

"The courtroom has been closed to the public - except the press - because this matter involves juveniles," explained the judge, whose name was Parsons as the nameplate on his high bench proclaimed.

The clerk stood and handed the judge a file folder of documents, then resumed his seat. Judge Parsons glanced through some of the legal papers, then peered up from them, lizard-like, asking, "Has the proposed agreement been accepted by all parties?"

"Yes," replied the 3 attorneys in unison again.

"Very well, let's begin." He cleared his throat. "I've studied the documents at length and feel that some modifications are in order which by statute is my prerogative."

Marty, Larson and Kliner exchanged worried expressions.

The judge continued. "The agreement calls for a sentence of 5 years to be imposed on all of the defendants. But taking into account the extenuating circumstances of the crime and the fact that several of the defendants are juveniles I felt that a certain leniency was called for."

Marty was about to angrily respond, but Larson grabbed his arm and kept him quiet.

"Therefore, it is the order of this Court," the judge went on, "that the 5 defendants - who are identified in the documents as persons A through E - are to receive 5 years imprisonment with 3 of the 5 to be on probation, leaving a total of 2 years to be served at the state facilities. The 6th defendant - identified as person F - is to serve 6 months at the County facilities due to his having only marginally participated in the crime." This elicited a controlled shout of delight and approval from the onlooking family members.

A person would have to wonder if a female judge would've applied such a light sentence since women experience the trauma and horror of rape with a much greater sensitivity.

"Your Honor," protested Kliner, "this is far less of a penalty than the prosecution had anticipated."

"I felt the modifications to be advised. It isn't the intention of this Court to ruin the entirety of the rest of the lives of these boys."

"What of the victim?" Larson asked. "She has been deprived of the rest of her life by these boys."

"And how would making the lives of the defendants more miserable help the victim?"

"What of justice?" demanded Kliner.

"What of leniency?" returned the judge. "We have to consider what is best for society as a whole - 6 hardened criminals or 6 reformed young men."

"And one dead girl still pleading for justice," Larson said.

Parsons gazed severely upon him. "Mr. attorney, if you have issues with the sentencing you know the proper venue in which to address them. Do so there."

"We shall, your honor," replied Kliner.

"But, remember counselors," the judge lectured, "the primary purpose for accepting the defendant's plea agreement was to avoid a trial and to keep private the identity of the victim. This will be done as I am now sealing this case and keeping all details of it from public scrutiny." He both signed and stamped a folder in which he placed legal documents of the proceedings. "This case is closed. Court is adjourned." He then got up and exited out the back.

Indeed, wealth had a great deal to do with the final outcome of this case! Although Marty, too, was wealthy, he could not compete with this group of the very affluent that confronted him.

It seemed that everybody arose at the same instant and began marching boisterously out of the courtroom. Amid the confusion and noise, the t.v. on-the-scene newsman Allan Morton charged through the crowd, almost bowling over a couple paralegals. In his mad race to capture the victim's hidden identity, Allan pounced first on the court reporter.

"Hello, I'm Allan Morton from local news," he professionally introduced himself to the prim young lady court reporter. "I was wondering if you could help me with a name I need for my evening news hour report."

Most professional court reporters are religiously protective of their data and documents, so her response was a simple, "I cannot help you with that."

"Really?" Allan tried. "I know it's all supposed to be secret but everyone here already knows the identities of the defendants; they all attend the local highschool. All I want to do is supply the identity of the victim for our t.v. viewers."

"Those records have been sealed by the Court."

"Just a technicality."

"It's a matter of privacy," said the court reporter.

"But the victim's dead."

"She still has her reputation."

"Ah, you women and your precious reputation!"

"Will there be anything else?"

Morton shook his head then sidled his way to the other end of the desk which was just beyond hearing range of the court reporter. He came upon the court clerk, a somewhat disheveled man in his early forties who was distracted by rearranging the stacks of documents around him.

"Quite a little mess, huh?" Morton remarked.

"Papers, papers, papers - that's what this job is all about. Is there something I can do for you?"

"I hope so. I'm Allan Morton of the local t.v. evening news. I'm covering this hearing and was hoping you could give me the name of who the victim was in this matter."

"Evening news, huh? Oh, yeah, I remember seeing you from time to time. What was it that you needed again?" asked the clerk.

"The victim's name. They never mentioned it."

"No, it's supposed to be some kind of a secret. But you're with the press so I guess it's all right."

The clerk picked out a piece of paper from a short pile and slid it over to Morton. The newsman eagerly devoured it.

"Sandra Kuhn," said the clerk. "That's her. She's the daughter of that famous bridge playing millionaire, Martin Kuhn."

"Oh yeah, the man who writes that bridge column with Omar Sharif."

"That's the one. He was here tonight at the hearing. Not Omar - Marty was."

The clerk took back the paper and returned it to the spot from where he'd taken it, saying, "I hope this helps."

"You have no idea!" beamed Morton, patting the man on the back then traipsing off in delight toward the side exit.

He strided toward his crew awaiting him at the door and, placing an arm around one of the female assistants, said, "Have I got the story of the year."

"What is it?" the woman excitedly asked.

"I want no chance of losing this one. You'll hear it like everybody else...when we go live on the air in 45 minutes."

Morton ushered his crew out the door and onto the courthouse steps to begin setting up for the fateful 5 p.m. news.

8

Judy and her step-family were seated together in their opulently furnished living room, watching the surround-sound, wide screen television, the most expensive and advanced money could buy at the time. They were aware of the sentencing that was to be carried out this day on Sandy's attackers and wanted to see the results. Judy sat as far away from the others as possible, positioning herself at the piano bench, protected behind the grand instrument as Todd tried to slither around her.

The Kuhn-Guilford family was not prepared for what was about to be shown on the television screen. And it occurred directly at the top of the hour, the first news story of the evening where an excited Allan Morton was waiting on the courthouse steps, microphone primed.

"Hello, this is on-the-spot news reporter Allan Morton coming from the steps of the Fulton County Courthouse in Atlanta, Georgia where the sentencing of the Sandy Springs 6 has just been completed. During coverage of this procedure, this reporter has managed to uncover the identity of the victim of the attack which left her dead at the hands of the 6 and it will be revealed here as an exclusive to this channel and cable network. The victim's name was Sandra Kuhn, daughter of a prominent Sandy Springs resident and well known bridge expert. The Sandy Springs 6 were charged with the rape and murder of the juvenile Miss Kuhn but during a plea agreement the charges were reduced to rape and battery. The sentences for Miss Kuhn's attackers weren't as harsh as expected, amounting to 2 years imprisonment and 3 years probation for 5 of the youth and 6 months jail time for the 6th. Today, the 6 boys finally had their day in court. And now the victim's identity has been revealed. This is Allan Morton for the 5 o'clock news."

"And when will Sandy get her day in court!" cried Judy, banging hard the piano keys.

The others wandered toward the television, gaping at it in terror.

"Your father is going to go out of his mind when he hears this," Bette called back to Judy, biting down on each word.

"Oh my God!" Phyllis intoned.

Todd, however, had a more offhand view, "Well, everyone at school suspected it was Sandy anyway. Not too many of them bought the idea that she was gone because she'd been shipped off to finishing school."

"Yeah, but now everyone will know for sure," noted Phyllis.

"Is that all you care about?" demanded Judy. "What about Sandy's good name?"

"Good name?" replied Phyllis. "She should've thought of that before jumping into a car with 6 drunken teenage boys."

"Yeah? Well, that's a chance I'm sure you wished you'd gotten yourself!" yelled Judy.

Todd walked over to Judy and placed a hand on her shoulder. "Calm down, she was only babbling as usual."

Judy flicked his hand away by a sharp flinch of her shoulder.

"And you," snapped Judy, "you would've changed places with any of those 6 who attacked Sandy."

"I believe you're right," Phyllis agreed. "He would have."

"Just as right as she was about you," returned Todd.

The verbal bloodletting was interrupted by the telephone in the living room ringing. Everyone stared at it in fear.

"I'm not going to answer it," said Phyllis. "It might be him - Marty."

Bette lumbered to the phone, picked up the receiver. Her face washed cold and white, then she slammed the receiver down.

"Well," she said "they've already begun. Now that they know it's Sandy for sure."

"What...what's already begun?" asked Phyllis.

"The obscene phone calls."

Everyone traded shocked expressions and then deflated in fear.

At that very moment, Marty and Larson knew nothing of what had just happened. They were entering a plush dining establishment in Atlanta named the Arbiter, where most of the attorney's ate at the end of the day. Marty and his attorney had been discussing legal matters in Larson's office until then and were not aware of the treachery that had just been committed on television.

This was Marty's first visit to the favorite eatery of the attorney set and he was caught off guard by the sudden silence choking the air the moment that he and Larson entered. Was it because Marty was a non-attorney? Surely they couldn't be that selective of patronage here.

Larson was just as surprised by the stranglehold of silence reminiscent of that which accompanied an unwanted character in Western movies when he entered the saloon or like in the old days when a woman of notoriety walked into the local beauty parlor during a gossip festival raging against her.

Both men froze in the center of the floor.

"Is my fly open or something?" Marty asked.

"I'm afraid you'll have to check that yourself," Larson told him.

"None of your lawyer friends have filed an arrest warrant against you, have they?" joked Marty.

"I don't think so."

"Do they always respond this way to new customers then? Some kind of tradition or something?"

"No. Something's wrong."

The maitre de stepped in to save the situation for the time being and approached the 2 shell shocked potential diners. "Good evening, gentlemen. This is the height of the dinner hour and you've caught us without any available tables. May I show you to the bar until a table becomes open?"

"Sure," said Larson. "But why has it become so silent all of a sudden?"

The maitre de evaded, saying, "Oh, it's just one of those lulls in talk that sometimes happen. You get used to them after you've been here as long as I have."

He started leading the 2 men toward the bar. "This way, please, while we prepare a table for you."

Crowd noise returned to normal as Marty and Larson took their seats at the bar. But this would only be a brief reprieve. As Marty lit up a cigar and ordered his usual cognac, he noted to his friend that the television above the bar was starting the 6 p.m. replay of the 5 o'clock news, the same telecast where his daughter's identity as the rape/murder victim was divulged. Of course, neither he nor Larson knew about this yet.

"Turn up the sound, will you," Larson instructed the bartender. "They might report on our case tonight."

The 6 o'clock report began with Morton's report. "Hello, this is on-the-spot news reporter Allan Morton coming from the steps of the Fulton County Courthouse in Atlanta, Georgia where the sentencing of the Sandy Springs 6 has just been completed. During coverage of this procedure, this reporter has managed to uncover the identity of the victim of the attack which left her dead at the hands of the 6 and it will be revealed here as an exclusive to this channel and cable network. The victim's name was Sandy Kuhn..."

Marty didn't hear any other words after that. He grabbed the edge of the bar in fury and remained in a mesmerized paralysis. Everything that had been sacrificed to keep Sandy's name from being mentioned had been for nothing. Murderers had been excused. Rapists had been given a light sentence. All so that a trial could be avoided to spare the victim's name from being publicized. And what happened!

"That bastard!" cried Marty before the newscast had even ended. "And he swore to me that her name would never be made public."

Larson sat speechless beside him.

"You said that all the top lawyers eat here," Marty said to Larson, eyeing the crowd with a vengeance. "Is that bastard Kliner here?"

"He's seated at his usual booth in the back by the wall where he eats in privacy."

"Huh," Marty scoffed, "a person like that should sit with his back to the wall and eat alone."

Marty got up and stalked toward Kliner with Larson tracing the big man's footsteps. The crowd once again was cloaked in silence. They wanted to hear what was going to transpire; they all knew the history of this case.

Marty arrived at Kliner's table, bracing angrily against it and boring his eyes into the district attorney's. Marty was a person of class and did not intend on putting on a show for the onlookers with shouting and table pounding. His normal voice could batter another person with words well enough. And Marty was a master at personal confrontation who took on the district attorney on a personal level.

"Did you see today's 5 o'clock news?" Marty asked Kliner.

"I'm afraid I did."

"So your word is worthless then?"

"I'm sorry, Mr. Kuhn, but the actions of the local cable television company are not within my purview."

"You led me to believe that they were. You swore that my daughter's name would never be released to the public."

"I cannot be responsible for every lawbreaker in the state, either. The person who gave her name on the air broke the law."

"What are you doing about him?"

"A warrant has been issued for his arrest."

"And what of the criminals who assaulted my daughter? Will they now get extended sentences because you broke your guarantee?"

"No, a plea deal is unbreakable."

"Unlike your word."

"Now, see here, Mr. Kuhn…"

"Don't bother," Marty said, turning from the table, "everyone here knows that nothing you say can be trusted."

He and Larson made their way back through the stunned diners and toward the front door.

"How can you stand to eat with these people?" Marty asked.

"You haven't tasted the coffee here yet," grinned Larson.

"That good, huh?"

They came to the front door.

"Well, I'm going to my club and get drunk and consider strangling the local D.A.," said Marty.

"As your attorney, I'll join you for the first part of your plan and advise you against the second," quipped Larson. In a serious mode, he grabbed Marty by the wrist, saying, "I didn't plan to lead you down the primrose path about keeping your daughter's name private. I…I…"

"It wasn't your fault. You thought you were dealing with an honest man."

They stepped out beneath the long canopy that protected the entrance way to the restaurant.

"Now what?" asked Marty. "About my daughter? Is there anything we can do?"

"I've already begun working on that. Yes, there is my friend. We sue. For a very large amount in damages."

"Sue who - the t.v. reporter? I doubt he has much money."

"Nope, we sue the cable company which has a great deal of money."

"You know, I don't really care about the money. I've already got lots of that. It's...letting them ruin my daughter's name. They should pay for it. Their irresponsibility has to be checked!"

"It will," replied Larson, putting a hand on his good friend's back as Marty's car was driven up to the curb by the attendant, "and they will pay."

9

Marty was at the head of the table the next night as the Kuhn/Guilford family sat for supper. His daughter, Judy, was on his right. Things were a lot different when he was home, as seldom as that was.

Bette was at the other end of the table, bracketed by her 2 children; and both sides were drawn.

The presentation of the evening newspaper to Marty by one of the servants set off the excitement. He opened the front page to be stared at by a photograph of his deceased daughter underneath a headline which blared: 6 SCHOOLBOYS SENTENCED IN RAPE AND ASSAULT OF SANDRA KUHN.

Marty crushed the paper closed then tossed it to the floor. "They used her yearbook picture! Her yearbook picture!"

"What?" asked Bette. "What are you bellowing about?"

"Sandy's face is plastered all over the front page - from her school yearbook!"

Todd leapt to the floor, scraped up the paper and spread it wide before him as he headed back to his seat. "Good likeness," he insensitively replied.

"Good what!" howled Marty, almost knocking Todd backwards with his voice.

"Nothing, nothing." Todd deflated into his seat.

"So now *she's* on trial," bemoaned Judy.

"Right," said Marty. "Just what I was afraid of."

"Are you going to do something about it?" challenged Bette.

"I already am. Bob Larson is drawing up a lawsuit against the cable company. It looks like he should add the newspaper publisher to it."

"Good, maybe we can make them pay through the nose for this," observed Bette.

"Is this what you think this is about?" Marty demanded.

"Why not? Make the most of it. Sandy's dead - nothing will change that."

Marty then detonated. "I don't ever want her name spoken in this house again! Ever!"

"Isn't that a little extreme?" Phyllis asked.

"Or even childish?" said Bette.

"I don't care. It's how I want it. Hearing her name is like dragging it through the mud."

"But..." tried Todd.

A deep stare from Marty shut him up. Then the telephone rang. Everyone except Marty stared at it in terror.

"What's wrong with all of you?" Marty demanded.

"It's...it's the phone," stammered Phyllis.

"Yes, I can hear it."

"We've been getting obscene phone calls about...about her since her name was given out," Bette struggled with the words.

"I expected this," Marty growled. He sprang up from his chair so quickly that it almost flew over backward.

Stomping to the phone, he snatched the receiver from the cradle. Everyone stiffened in his chair, awaiting the outburst. There was none. They all fell back as one.

Instead of a shouting confrontation, Marty had a civil discussion then returned to his seat.

"What was that about?" Bette asked.

"My attorney. He called to let me know that the trial against the cable company gets underway in 6 weeks."

"That's pretty quick, isn't it?" asked Bette, eagerly.

"The cable company wants to get this over with quickly."

"Good, maybe they're ready to settle and we'll get a nice payment from them!" chimed Bette.

"So you can buy another million dollar jade lamp stand for your room at the expense of my daughter's life?"

"Oh, Marty!"

Marty got up and left the table. Judy followed him to the ornately decorated and luxuriously furnished living room where

Marty slowly paced and his daughter settled into an overstuffed armchair. The others stayed in place at the table, tearing into the remains of dinner like carrion crows.

"Aren't you hungry?" Marty asked Judy.

"I've had enough. Anyway, I can't eat with them."

"No, I guess not."

"I can't live with them either. I tried, but..."

"That's originally why I thought you would be better off living with your mother."

"No, I can't go back there! I can't! She's a monster."

"I wasn't thinking of sending you back to her."

"Why can't you and I go live somewhere? You have that penthouse in Longboat Key."

"It would never work. I'm out of town too often on business or at bridge tournaments."

"Well, what then?" Judy asked.

"We need to find a good school for you," Marty suggested.

"Not a finishing school! That's what Bette is planning for me."

"No, not one of those. A private boarding school of some type."

"Which one?"

"Tell you what - you pick one out. Go to the one you like. Anywhere. Cost doesn't matter."

"Me? What do I know about boarding schools?"

"About as much as I do. But I'll bet that someone at the public library can help you. At least to get started," Marty suggested.

"Okay. I'll go check that out tomorrow. But I wish..." she abruptly stopped herself.

"You wish?"

"That...that she was here. She always helped me with things like this."

"I should've done this in the first place - sent the 2 of you to a good boarding school after the divorce. Now, well now..."

"I'm sure you did the best you could."

"For who I am, yes I did. I'm not a natural family man. I know that. It's one reason I got married again, to have a ready-made family for the 2 of you. That didn't work out so well, did it?."

"Bette and her kids hate us," Judy affirmed.

"They don't think much of me, either."

"So, why did Bette marry you?"

"For the money."

"Did you know that?"

"Pretty much." Marty nodded. "But, back then, she was a lot prettier."

"Hard to believe that."

"She became addicted to cheese cake. It's my fault. I took her to a restaurant in Atlanta that's known for its cheese cake."

"Don't ever take me there," Judy said with a smile.

"I don't think you'll be in Atlanta much longer."

The telephone rang. Marty went to answer it. After a couple minutes he hung up. "Got to go," he told Judy. "They need someone to sit in a special bridge tournament tonight."

"Okay. Good luck, Dad."

Marty walked over and patted her on the shoulder before heading toward the door.

And Judy sadly said to herself as she slowly walked toward her room, "Who's ever going to call me Jude again - now that Sandy's gone?"

10

Judy left for her new school several weeks before the first trial seeking to restore her sister's innocence was to begin. She escaped the control of her psychotic stepfamily and her sadistic mother for all time and kept up a periodic contact with her father who remained emotionally distant but nonetheless concerned with her welfare.

Marty had paid all of the costs for the new school to which Judy was arriving this cold, Vermont winter afternoon. The schoolhouse itself was one large, round building of dubious architectural style. It was surrounded by a number of smaller, more normal appearing "out" buildings where some of the craft classes were held. This was supposed to be a highly progressive school based on an educational concept that originated in France. What exactly the concept was supposed to entail was never very clearly defined other than promoting the open-minded search for knowledge in an unencumbered setting which was also a process not clearly defined.

In reality, it was a place where the students could both enjoy almost unlimited freedom but also have access to special educational opportunities unbound by the normal restrictions of schedule and time. This freedom was one of the reasons why Judy chose this progressive school to attend. Another was the wide curriculum of crafts taught here by professionals in each field, particularly weaving and pottery making. She didn't know, however, how secluded the location was, set in the barren fields many miles from the nearest town.

Judy's cab drove up to the entrance of the great round building where the administration offices also were.

"Well, here it is," said the cabbie. "The great house they call it."

"In the middle of nowhere, too."

"Are you sure you want to stay here?" asked the cabbie.

"I've got nowhere else to go."

Judy handed him her fare and a generous tip, then started from the car. The cabbie got out and carried the one suitcase she had over to her . "Is this all you got, miss?"

"I had everything else shipped ahead."

"Okay, then. Good luck." The cabbie tipped his hat then headed back to the car.

When he drove off, Judy felt as alone as she'd ever felt. It was quiet and brooding here, almost gothic in setting; she liked that part of it. Judy started up the long flagstone path to the office entrance. There wasn't any signage for direction but there was no alternative pathway. Besides, the office entrance just looked like one.

Judy walked up to the door and went inside without knocking. It was a small, one room office furnished with a large desk and several filing cabinets. A young woman named Marla was behind the desk and looked up from her paperwork at the new arrival, not particularly interested or friendly of appearance. Marla was young and pretty in a garish way and immediately looked upon Judy as a rival, something which the newcomer quickly sensed as most any woman would.

Judy set down her suitcase and took a seat in one of the two wooden arm chairs before the desk. "And you must be Judy Kuhn," said Marla, flipping a form over with the tip of her pencil.

"Must I?"

"Well, you're in her seat," Marla aptly returned.

"You're right," Judy demurred.

"I always am," Marla professed.

"Nice to know."

"I'm Mala Bates, one of the 2 directors of this establishment. I see you've come alone. Adventurous?"

"Abandoned."

"But not forgotten. Someone's paid a great deal to see that you're well taken care of while here."

"What does well taken care of mean?" asked Judy.

"You'll be supplied with all of the best craft materials you'll ever want and be individually instructed in their proper use. We were assured by a man named Marty that there'd be help to pay if you weren't."

"My main reason for coming here was the pottery and weaving programs."

"You're lucky," Marla said, "I'm the pottery instructor. You'll get the best training in how to use the wheel, apply glaze and control proper firing techniques."

"I'll look forward to that."

"You've arrived here in the middle of things, though. We're just finishing construction on an addition to the main building. That's to house the new type of clientele we're now accepting."

"We're adding juvenile wards of the state to our student body," Marla replied.

"You mean young criminals. You didn't care to mention that in your sales brochures," noted Judy.

"It's a relatively new development. We needed the extra income to keep this place going."

"It's still a school, right?" Judy earnestly asked.

"Of course. While you can't get a regular diploma here you will obtain a GED that will be accepted by most major colleges. We are quite progressive here."

"Yes, an experimental program, I know. But now with a criminal element added to the student body."

"They have a right to an education, too."

"And committing murder sometimes, too."

"My, that's a little drastic isn't it?"

"My older sister was raped and murdered by a group of her classmates. And they were given a slap on the wrist for what they did. I might even see one of them show up here."

"Uh, not likely," said Marla, flipping through the papers on her desk with the friendly tip of her pencil again. "I see you're from Georgia. Out-of-state kids wouldn't be likely to be transferred here."

"I'm from out-of-state. Well, I'll let you know if I see any of those out-of-state delinquents around," replied Judy with a smirk.

"My boyfriend Roger Parker and I have built this place together and don't plan on letting it deteriorate into a reform school."

Judy peered at the photo on Marla's desk of her and Roger in a sideways embrace on a beach somewhere.

"That must be Roger," noticed Judy.

"That's him. And don't get any ideas, either."

"Look, I just turned 14 a couple months ago. And I sure didn't come here looking for a relationship."

"Nobody does. It sometimes just happens."

"Not to me."

"Don't think so little of yourself," Marla noted. "You know as well as I that you'd be a good catch."

"Better make sure I'm not a barracuda."

At that moment, almost on cue, Roger Parker blew in through the back door that led to the main part of the building. He was tall, handsome, in his late 20's and sported a dashing black mustache, certainly an attraction for any impressionable young woman. And he had the alluring voice to match.

Glancing at length at Judy, he noted, "Ah, this must be the young Miss Kuhn we've been expecting."

"Yes, the *young* Miss Kuhn," replied Marla, emphasizing the word young.

"Has Marla acclimated you to things here?" Roger asked Judy directly with a tone that made one feel he was talking in a way especially to you.

Marla strategically answered instead of Judy. "Yes, I have acclimated her, Roger, to the most important rules to be observed in our establishment."

"Good, then I'm just in time to give her a guided tour of the facilities."

"It would be good to remind yourself of the rules of our institution as well," Marla spoke to Roger. "Particularly the one against fraternizing with the students, the *much* younger students."

"Naturally," said Roger. "And I expect you to adhere to that restriction as well with these new male students being admitted."

"Certainly, dear."

The infighting was making Judy feel like she was back home with her stepfamily. Roger slid his hand around the back of Judy's chair and practically raised her from her seat as she stood to his touch. "But there's no harm in a simple tour of our facilities. And who is better than me."

"Keep it simple," advised Marla.

"But thorough," he said, snatching up Judy's suitcase.

The 2 started out of the office but Marla detained them a moment longer, telling Roger, "You might be interested in knowing, dear, that Miss Kuhn recently turned 14 years old."

"Then we must throw her a belated birthday party. See if you can scout up some candles for her, will you?"

Judy and Roger headed off on their tour of the facilities which were then in use by the student body during this middle portion of the day. The girl students ogled Mr. Parker and the male students sought Judy's attention in the usual inane ways.

Judy and her guide visited the art room, pottery throwing and glazing area, the kiln, and the spacious weaving stations. They also looked in the gym and basic classrooms before ending up in the student dormitory on the 2nd level. Judy's room was a small apartment with 2 beds, 2 desks and 2 dressers, it being fitted for double occupancy. The room was empty at first, but the awkward privacy was abruptly ended by the sudden appearance of Karen Moore, the girl who was to be Judy's roommate. She was one year older than Judy but of very similar size and overall build.

"Well, it looks like you've received a reprieve," Roger said to Judy.

"I didn't know I needed one," was the naive reply. Although Judy was astute when evading the advances of the more obvious type of molester, she wasn't nearly as perceptive when in the presence of a well-polished seducer.

Roger quickly introduced the 2 girls and departed to attend to loud shouting that came from somewhere below.

"Just the new boys trying to kill each other again," Karen dryly noted.

"As long as they keep it among themselves," smiled Judy.

"That's a pleasant thought: those maniacs killing off one another and leaving us alone."

"Well, I'm new to this place - just arrived."

"I noticed. You weren't here before."

"I could've been hiding in the closet all this time," Judy returned.

"No, that's where I hide. I probably would've noticed you in there."

"Maybe not - if you didn't turn on the light."

"Our closets aren't that big," responded Karen. "We would've bumped into each other sooner or later."

Judy got serious. "How long have you been here?"

"About 6 months. It wasn't so bad until they let those delinquents in."

The increased shouting from below rolled along the bedroom floor.

"What's even worse," added Karen, "is that Roger - the owner - is almost as bad as they are. A real creep."

"His girlfriend doesn't seem much better."

"Marla's a bitch! But she is a great teacher. Knows everything there is to know about pottery."

"Maybe because she's had to replace so much cup-ware after throwing it all at Roger," Judy observed.

"Hey, that's good. You're sharp!"

The noises from below continued

"What do we do about that?" Judy asked.

Karen dragged a chair over to the door and wedged it beneath the knob, "First we do this. The lousy lock is broken."

Karen then strided across the room to a phonograph on a stand and turned it on, "Then we do this to cover up the shouting and screaming. Hope you like the Beatles."

The opening words of a famous Beatles song blared from the speakers. "Hey, Jude - don't be afraid..."

Judy fell back. Was it a message from her sister Sandy? If only Judy could find at least one place in her life where she *could* sleep at night without terror. This did not seem to be that place.

11

As Judy acclimated herself to her new, though familiar environment, the first trial that was being held to rescue Sandy's reputation was beginning in Atlanta. Demonstrations raged outside the court-house on the initial day of proceedings. Two sides were pitted against each other. One cried out for the release of the 6 imprisoned attack-ers of Sandy Kuhn and the other group called for the passage of the Equal Rights Amendment - being hotly debated in 1972 - and for the expansion of women's rights and freedoms.

Chants from the opposing sides washed over Marty and his attor-ney Larson as they strode up the flight of stairs and into the court-house. The cries could barely be heard once inside the protected halls of the fortified building.

Spectators had packed the inside of the courtroom already and both sides of the legal matter anxiously prepared to face each other with the same ferocity as those groups on the steps outside.

After all of the initial preliminaries had been taken care of, Mr. Larson arose to give his synopsis of their argument to the judge whom it had been agreed would be the sole arbiter of the case; at the defendant's insistence. The charge being leveled against the Kerner Cable Corporation by the plaintiff, Martin Kuhn, was invasion of privacy and the damages being sought were one million dollars. But in essence the trial was primarily being held to vindicate the good name of the victim, Sandy Kuhn.

(presented in a modified deposition form)

Larson: Your honor, the plaintiff will show that in direct violation of the laws of the state of Georgia and its Supreme Court prohibiting disclosing the identity of a female rape victim the defendant did wilfully divulge the identity of Sandy Kuhn to the public on one of its nightly newscasts, causing irreparable harm to the family of said victim for which damages of one million dollars is being sought.

With that brief introduction, Larson returned to his seat. Judge Winslow Bain, a hefty man in his mid 50's peered down from the same high bench from which the 6 youths who'd assaulted Miss Kuhn had been sentenced. He addressed the defense attorney, "Miss. Shipton?"

Penny Shipton was the attorney for the defense, a young, perfectly coiffed and sharply attired advocate for corporate rights as well a strong supporter of the then popular Equal Rights Amendment.

Shipton: I prefer Ms. Shipton, your honor. We contend that divulging the name of the victim was a matter of first amendment rights and freedom of the press and that this suit dangerously verges on a frivolous undertaking. I request a summary judgment be granted on our behalf.

Judge Bain: Request denied. Any further motions?

Shipton : No, your honor.

Shipton then resumed her seat.

Judge Bain: Call your first witness for the appellant.

Larson called Bryce Grundmeyer to the stand, a tall man in his mid 40's of slim build and sporting a headful of curly red hair and prominent red mustache. He was president and general manager of the news corporation that broadcast the offending story which divulged Miss Kuhn's identity. Taking the oath, he then sat in the witness stand.

Larson approached him like a boxer in a ring.

Larson: What is your job title?

Bryce: I am CEO and station manager of TV-Atlanta which is owned by Kerner Cable Corporation.

Larson: You're the boss at TV-Atlanta, right? There's no one above you?

Bryce: At this station I am the boss, yes.

Larson: Is providing what is called breaking news part of the services your business delivers?

Bryce: A very large part of it. We specialize in local news.

Larson: And this was the service you provided when you revealed the identity of Miss Kuhn on your nightly news?

Bryce: Yes. It was newsworthy.

Larson: Ah, newsworthy. What does that mean?

Bryce: It means something that is taking place in the community at large that it is important that the citizens know about.

Larson: I see. So you considered it important that the public know the identity of a juvenile, female rape victim on the 5 o'clock news that particular evening.

Bryce: Certainly. It was breaking news.

Larson: But why was only the victim's name released?

Bryce: Because the defendants were juveniles and it is against the law to reveal the identities of juveniles in such a situation.

Larson: Well, that confuses me greatly Mr. Grundmeyer. The victim was also a juvenile. But you decided it was all right to provide her identity.

Bryce: Yes. She was deceased and the public had a right to know her identity. A deceased person does not have any rights.

Larson: Not true, according to the Supreme Court of Georgia. Are you aware that it is a crime in this state to divulge the identity of a female rape or murder victim whether the individual is dead or alive?

Bryce: I...I'm not sure.

Larson: Mr. Grundmeyer - please! Not sure? Surely as a professional journalist living in this state this law must be known to you. Otherwise you would have to be determined as terribly incompetent. You know, of course, that ignorance of a law is no excuse for breaking it.

Bryce: Yes, I am aware of that and of the law you mentioned.

Larson: But you chose to ignore it.

Bryce: Yes, in the public interest.

Larson: And maybe for some private interests as well?

Bryce: I don't understand.

Larson: Weren't some of the juveniles who were convicted of Miss Kuhn's attack the children of wealthy and powerful individuals?

Bryce: You might say so.

Larson: Oh, I do say so. But for propriety, I'll not mention their names unless I have to. But the father of one of the accused's is an attorney who helped establish the Kerner Cable Network, correct?

Bryce: Even if some powerful people might be involved in the matter - so what?

Larson: Could it be that by making the victim the center of attraction all eyes would be taken from her attackers and placed solely onto the victim? Especially if their names - names of the attackers - were not made public? Could that be the case?

Bryce: It's your theory.

Larson: A good one, too. At least 3 of the attacker's parents are major advertisers on your television station, are they not?

Attorney Shipton : Objection, you honor. Relevance.

Judge Bain: Sustained. You have no foundation Mr. Larson.

Larson (to the witness): Would you agree that privacy is an important right, Mr. Grundmeyer?

Bryce: Yes.

Larson: Mr. Grundmeyer, didn't you earlier say something to the effect that divulging the victim's name wasn't injurious because, after all, she was dead?

Bryce: Yes, something to that effect. And I still feel that way. How could a dead person be denied privacy?

Larson: And what of the plaintiff and his family? Did you not impinge upon their privacy when you published the name of the victim on television? That's the central point of this lawsuit.

Bryce: All we were doing was covering an ongoing news event.

Larson: I see, so you determined that it was important that the public know the name of the victim.

Bryce: Certainly. A major event was in the process of happening.

Larson: I just cannot understand your logic Mr. Grundmeyer. Not at all. You thought it was important for the public to know the name of the innocent victim of rape and murder. But you didn't think it was important for the public to know the identities of the individuals who perpetrated these heinous acts! Even when they still might be loose in this community you're trying so hard to protect.

Bryce: They were juveniles.

Larson: So was the victim. Why are the assailants allowed more rights than the victim?

Bryce: I can't answer that.

Larson: Maybe I have an idea. Let's look into basic human nature.

Bryce: If you wish.

Larson: What do you think public opinion would be if the name of the victim of a sexual crime was released to the public but not the names of the offenders?

Bryce: I can't say.

Larson: Come on, Mr. Grundmeyer, public opinion is your business. You know full well that in the scenario I just propounded that the victim would be made into the guilty party, the one who provoked the crime.

Bryce: I don't know that.

Larson: And in the case of Sandy Kuhn she would be judged guilty simply by her gender. Guilty by being female.

Bryce: I...I don't see that.

Larson: Well, let me show you the image you presented to the public, Mr. Grundmeyer. Your newscast made it quite clear that the victim was 1 female alone in the company of 6 drunken teenage boys. What kind of picture does that draw for the general public! Exactly the picture you wanted to paint in order to take all eyes off the offenders because some of their parents were huge advertisers on your television station.

Bryce: No!

Larson: Yes! Yes, Mr Grundmeyer. All that Sandy Kuhn wanted from those boys that night was a ride home!

Bryce: So?

Larson: You made it appear that she wanted much more than that.

There was a pause as Larson turned and walked back to his desk. He picked up a folder of papers, quickly scanned the documents inside, then stalked back to the witness.

Larson: Did you read the coroner's report that was filed on this case?

Bryce: No.

Larson: No! Really! Too bad, you missed a vital piece of evidence. Would you like to know what that was?

Bryce: Go ahead.

Larson: According to the coroner, the victim - Sandy Kuhn - was a virgin prior to being raped by her attackers on the night in question. Did you know that! Did you!

Bryce: Uh, no.

Larson: Don't you think that this is a piece of information you might have wanted to convey to your viewing public at the same time you released,

illegally, the identity of the victim?

Bryce: I...I...I don't know.

Larson: Don't know, or don't care! Because if that bit of information had been released the victim would not look like some long time whorewho was just out for another fun night. Don't you think?

Bryce: Providing information on the victim's background wasn't my concern.

Larson: But that's exactly what you did! You left your viewers with the impression that the victim was some kind of slut out for a good time with 6 of her classmates. And if you would have let your audience know about

the coroner's report, verifying the victim's prior virginity, public opinion might have viewed her differently.

Bryce: I guess...maybe.

Larson: Maybe! Doesn't the news industry have a cannon of ethics by which it claims to govern itself?

Bryce: Yes, as do most industries.

Larson: You even have them in writing; I just glanced through some of that code. Do you by chance recall your own industry's recommendation about releasing the name of a juvenile female victim of rape to the public?

Bryce: In general, yes.

Larson: The news broadcasting industry's canon of ethics directly advises against releasing the name of a juvenile female rape victim.

Bryce: That can be interpreted in different ways.

Larson: Seriously! How can that be interpreted in more than one way?

Bryce: I haven't considered the matter.

Larson: Clearly. So, how exactly did you follow this code of ethics that advises against releasing the name of a female victim of rape?

Bryce: As best I could.

Larson: By ignoring it you mean. And, tell me, what is a different way to interpret the words "advisable not to release names of juvenile female rape victims to the public" than not to release the names of juvenile female rape victims to the public?

Bryce: I don't know of any.

Larson: Because there isn't any. Now, the person who first revealed the victim's name is Allan Morton, your on-the-scene reporter. Do you know if he is aware of your industry's code of ethics?

Bryce: You'll have to ask him.

Larson: You can be sure I will. Did you direct him to release the name of the victim on that nightly newscast?

Bryce: No, I did not.

Larson: Did he alert you beforehand that he was going to do so?

Bryce: No, he did not.

Larson: He didn't need your permission to undertake such a potentially litigious act?

Bryce: No, most reporters in the field have wide latitude in their method.

Larson: Even so, you are aware, are you not, that if an employee of a corporation such as yours releases information that results in a lawsuit that the company which employs him is also liable?

Bryce: Of course.

Larson: And, being aware of the contents of that defamatory newscast which revealed the juvenile victim's identity, you chose to rerun the same program an hour later?

Bryce: I did.

Larson: Knowing what it contained, you ran the piece again?

Bryce: I said so.

Larson: So, you compounded the crime.

As the witness tried to stammer a reply, Larson turned from him.

Larson: Your honor, I have no more questions for this witness.

The defense then took over questioning Mr. Grundmeyer.

Shipton: Only a few questions. Mr. Grundmeyer, did you use your best judgment in rerunning the telecast of the 5 o'clock news during which the victim's identity was divulged?

Bryce: I did.

Shipton: Was it your intention to harm the victim, her family or those associated with them?

Bryce: It was not.

Shipton: Was it your intention to protect the identities of certain families who advertised on your television station?

Bryce: It never occurred to me.

Shipton: No further questions.

Judge Bain: Mr. Larson, do you have any redirect?

Mr. Larson faced the witness again.

Larson: Yes. Mr. Grundmeyer, are you aware now and were you aware at the time that after the sentencing proceedings were concluded the judge had all records sealed because the matter involved juveniles?

Bryce: Yes, I was always aware of this.

Larson: What is the purpose of sealing court records? Isn't it to keep the information contained in them private and out of public view?

Bryce: Yes.

Larson: Would that information include the name of the victim?

Bryce: Uh...well...I...I would think probably so.

Larson: No, Mr. Grundmeyer - definitely so! The records had been sealed in order to protect the victim's name as well as the others involved. Yet you felt it your right to ignore this legal requirement and divulge the victim's name anyway?

Bryce: I...I...guess so.

Larson: You guess so? Guess so? No, you did so, Mr. Grundmeyer. Against the wishes of the Court you released information that was deemed private and thereby broke even another statute of the law.

With that, Larson concluded his examination of Bryce Grund-meyer. The defense didn't have any other questions of him, and then the newsman Allan Morton was called to the stand. Prior to that, the judge called a 15 minute recess.

12

Resumption of the trial. Allan Morton is on the witness stand.

Larson: You are Allan Morton, the television newscaster who was first to identify to the public the victim who is the subject of this lawsuit?

Morton: I sure am.

Larson: How did you learn of the victim's identity?

Morton: Simple. After the 6 were sentenced I walked over to the clerk of the court and asked to see the indictment.

Larson: And Miss Kuhn's name was on the indictment, describing her as the victim.

Morton: That's right. There wasn't anything illegal in the way I obtained her name.

Larson: Were there any other names on the indictment?

Morton: Naturally. Witnesses, attorneys - you know.

Larson: And the names of the 6 accused? Were they on the indictment?

Morton: Of course.

Larson: But you didn't mention any of their names on the news-cast when you identified the victim.

Morton: No.

Larson: Why not?

Morton: First - they were juveniles. Second - there wasn't as much interest in their identities.

Larson: Why would it matter if they were juveniles?

Morton: You know as well as I do that the identities of juveniles are

prohibited from being released.

Larson: But you felt perfectly free to release the name of the victim

who was a juvenile.

Morton: For the same reasons given by Mr. Grundmeyer. Dead

people have no rights.

Larson: Don't their families have rights?

Morton: Rights to do what?

Larson: Privately mourn their dead for one thing.

Morton: And television viewers have rights to the news no matter who it affects.

Larson: You and Mr. Grundmeyer might be interested in the court's findings in a 1926 case then.

Morton: Go ahead. I've got nothing else to do.

Larson: The case was Havermayer vs. Havermayer. A woman laid to rest her deceased second husband in the same tomb with her deceased first husband. The two legal children of the woman's first husband sued their mother for trespass and infringement of privacy rights by laying the second husband in the same vault. They won their suit.

Morton: So?

Larson: The court ruled that the mother had to remove the second husband from the tomb because his presence was offensive not just to the children but also to their dead father. Their dead father.

Morton: Where did you dig that up?

Larson: A book of law. The same kind which states that a victim and his survivors have rights and these are rights that you have violated.

Morton: I have rights, too. First amendment and freedom of the Press.

Larson: Not in this case. Your rights cease when you break the law. According to the Supreme Court of this state you broke the law when you divulged the identity of a juvenile female rape victim.

Morton: The story was news. I reported it as is my right and responsibility.

Larson: You said that you obtained the name of the victim from the court

clerk.

Morton: That's right.

Larson: Was this before or after the sentencing of the accused?

Morton: Like I told you earlier, it was after.

Larson: I see. And this would've been after the presiding judge officially sealed the records.

Morton: But the records I used were the indictment - public records.

Larson: No. They may have been public records before sentencing, but not after. Not after the judge sealed the records of this case. You have no legal excuse. You used legal information illegally.

Morton: I plead freedom of the press in any case.

Larson: What about a person's right to privacy?

Morton: First amendment and freedom of the press supersedes that right.

Larson: And what about your right to determine public opinion? We once had A discussion about that at a protest you were covering. Remember?

Morton: Sort of.

Larson: At the time, I asked you if you were prepared to face the con-sequences for revealing the victim's name and directing public sentiment on the matter. Well, this is your day of judgment.

Morton: Is it?

Larson: You clearly broke the law, existing Georgia law, prohibitingthe release of a juvenile rape victim's identity. Or does being a newsreporter raise you above the law.

Morton: No comment.

Larson: Ironic, hearing that from a newsman.

Morton: And I stand by it.

Larson: Did you read the coroner's report concerning this case?

Morton: No.

Larson: Not very good research. Or a purposeful neglect?

Morton: What.

Larson: The coroner proved that the victim was a virgin before her attack.That information would've ruined your attempt to highlight her as a tramp or whore and to make her seem the guilty party. So you kept it secret.

Morton: Why would I want to do that?

Larson: To make the true guilty parties seem more sympathetic. And improve your ratings maybe.

Morton: You have no right to...

Larson spun away from the witness. "I have no more questions for this person, your honor."

Judge Bain: Does the defense wish to cross-examine?

Shipton: No, your honor.

Judge Bain: Does the plaintiff have another witness to call?

Larson: Yes, your honor. I call to the stand Jennet Williams.

Jennet Williams, a prim young woman modestly dressed and wearing a light amount of makeup took the stand. The oath was given and Mr. Larson began his direct examination.

Larson: Miss, Williams, or is it Ms?

Williams: I'm a conservative girl so I still use Miss.

Larson: Conservative and professional. Tell us your profession please.

Williams: I'm a court reporter.

Larson: How long have you worked in this profession?

Williams: Going on 8 years.

Larson: Were you the court reporter assigned to cover the sentencing of the 6 juveniles who attacked Miss Kuhn?

Williams: Yes, I was.

Larson: Did at any time the previous witness on the stand, Allan Morton, speak to you at those proceedings?

Williams: Yes.

Larson: For what purpose?

Williams: After the sentencing had concluded he approached my desk and asked me to supply him with the identity of the victim.

Larson: How did you respond?

Williams: I told him that I wouldn't give him that information. It was private and the judge had just sealed the records.

Larson: You said that to him?

Williams: Not in those exact words, but the meaning was the same.

Larson: So he understood that the records he sought were private and that the judge had sealed them?

Williams: Yes, I told him that.

Larson: Thank you, Miss Williams, that is all I have.

Judge Bain: Call your next witness.

Larson: We rest, your honor.

The defense had no questions for Miss Williams.

Judge Bain: Miss Shipton, call your first witness to the stand.

Shipton: It's still Ms Shipton, your honor. The defense calls to the stand Edward Marks.

The court clerk who'd attended the sentencing of the 6 juvenile attackers took the stand and was sworn in.

Shipton: You are Edward Marks, clerk of the court?

Marks: Yes, I am.

Shipton: You were the clerk during the proceedings in which the 6 juveniles were sentenced?

Marks: I was.

Shipton: Was there a time when Allan Morton approached you and requested documents that were pertinent to that case?

Marks: Yes there was.

Shipton: Did you supply him with the documents he sought?

Marks: Yes, I thought they were public records.

Shipton: Mr. Morton didn't use any force to obtain the records from you did he?

Marks: No, he didn't.

Shipton: You let him have them without any coercion.

Marks: Yes.

Shipton: Why? I mean, why didn't you stop him like the court reporter did?

Marks: It's like I said earlier. I felt they were public records.

Shipton: Thank you, Mr. Marks. I have no more questions.

Judge Bain: Mr. Larson, would you like to cross-examine?

Larson: Yes, your honor.

He approaches the witness.

Larson: You said that there was a time when Mr. Morton asked you for documents relating to the case at hand.

Marks: Yes.

Larson: The defense neglected to ask you at what time it was that Mr. Morton asked you for these documents.

Marks: Well, I wasn't looking at my watch at that moment.

Larson: No, what I mean is what time was it in relation to the proceedings. It was after sentencing, correct?

Marks: Yes.

Larson: And it was after the judge had sealed these selfame records.

Marks: Yes.

Larson: So, Mr. Morton had asked you for documents that the judge had already sealed from the public.

Marks: Yeah, but I didn't know I was doing anything wrong. I didn't.

Larson: No, you may not have, Mr. Marks. But Mr. Morton did.

Shipton: I object, your honor.

Judge Bain: Overruled.

Larson: I have no more questions.

Judge Bain: Does the defense?

Shipton: No, your honor. And we rest our case.

Judge Bain: Then is the plaintiff prepared to make a closing statement?

Larson: Yes, your honor.

Judge Bain: Very well, closing statements will be made following the Lunch recess. Court will resume at 2 P.M.

13

Marty and Larson had lunch together at a small, local bar and grille during the break. While Mr. Larson dined on a corned beef and cabbage sandwich, Marty ordered a snifter of cognac to enjoy with his havana.

"The other side didn't put up much of a defense," Marty noted.

"I didn't expect they would. The cable company clearly broke the law. That's why they insisted on a non-jury trial; so a judge would make the ruling."

"You mean it's more likely that a jury might have ruled against them?"

"Very probably," said Larson. "You can never tell what a jury will do, but in this case a jury probably would've burned the defense."

"So what are our chances of winning with a judge?"

"Still better than average. The written law is on our side. But I expect that if we win the case it'll be appealed."

"Then what?" asked Marty.

"Continue fighting as long as you want to."

"There's something I don't understand about what happened in court before the lunch recess," said Marty. "You didn't call the court clerk as a witness but questioned him after the other side did."

"Tactics, my friend," said Larson. "He wouldn't have helped our case so I didn't call him. The defense called him because they wanted to make it look like revealing the sealed documents was the clerk's fault and that Morton was blameless."

"Ah."

"The defense wants to make a test case of this. This isn't a simple local matter now. It's a battle between free speech of the Press and the individual's right to privacy. There isn't any precedent in the books."

"Which means?"

"It may go all the way to the top."

"The Supreme Court?"

"That's the one," Larson said with a smile, then chomped into the thick corned beef sandwich. "I'll recommend another attorney to argue the case for you if it should come to any appellate level hearing."

"Couldn't you handle it?"

"Yes, but I wouldn't give you the best representation. Someone with Appellate Court experience would be much better."

"Thanks. I appreciate that. Who do you have in mind?"

"Lawton Philips," replied Larson. "A good man."

Marty nodded thoughtfully. "I've heard of him." Then he asked, "I've got a strange question for you," said Marty. "You told Bryce while he was on the stand that you'd ask Morton if he knew about the news industry's code of ethics."

"Okay, and...?"

"You never asked Morton that question."

"I lied," Larson joked. "No, really, it was unimportant."

"And another thing. It hasn't got anything to do with anything - but what was all that business in court about Miss and Ms? Ms is a word now?"

"It has to do with the women's liberation movement and the Equal Rights Amendment which they're promoting. They feel that since an unmarried male isn't noted as such by his prefix neither should an unmarried female. Thus, Ms instead of Miss."

"Kind of makes sense. But why don't they get a better word than Ms? Sounds more like a description for a bumble bee."

"Maybe we should suggest that to Ms. Shipton," Larson lightly said.

"Sure, let's think up an alternative for Ms. In the meantime, I'm going to get a refill on my cognac."

At two o'clock they returned to court for the last segment of the hearing - final arguments. The defense had very little to say, simply repeating that they had the first amendment and freedom of the Press as reason to legally explain their activity. Larson had little to say as well, observing that the defendants had broken Georgia law prohibiting revealing the identity of a juvenile female victim of a rape and this was "cut and dried" as the term is.

When all arguments were completed, Larson stood before the bench. "Your honor," he began, "both sides have now had their day in court so to speak. I at this time seek relief and damages in this matter favorable to the plaintiff."

Judge Bain: Your case in this matter is very strong. In fact, the law is quite clear and it is as clear that the defendants are in violation of the law. Therefore, your request for relief and damages is granted.

Shipton: Your honor, we intend to appeal your finding.

Judge Bain: As is your right. But this court is adjourned.

The ruling by the judge was appealed by the broadcasting corporation and was next heard by the Supreme Court of Georgia. The justices listened to the same arguments and came to the same conclusion as the lower court had - that the Cable Broadcast Corporation violated Georgia law and was liable for damages. This was in 1973 and it brought about another appeal, this time to the Supreme Court of the United States. Because this was a topic of pressing interest, the Supreme Court expedited the matter and agreed to hear oral arguments in the coming November of 1974. The necessary preliminaries had been fulfilled and the true battle for justice was soon to be made in the austere environment of the chambers of the Supreme Court.

In the time in between, Marty finally dissolved his tortuous marriage and relieved himself of the company of Bette and her seriously deranged children but only at great monetary cost. Also during this time, Judy received excellent instruction in weaving and ceramic design from experts in these fields but received very little in the way of formal education. However, she did escape the Great House with a GED certificate after a couple of years. At this place, she also learned how to evade and avoid the hostile pursuit of libido driven young delinquents and learned who to accept protection from in this endeavor, resulting in a number of casual and luckily not tragic relationships for her. If only she could've received guidance from her older sister Sandy instead of from strangers.

Judy became lost in mind and body after her sudden graduation from the Great House and found what she thought was a path to flight in the company of a young man visiting from Brazil who had been introduced to her one cold Vermont night at a pizza parlor by a friend from school. His name was Pepe Reyes. He was 22, tall, dark, slender and handsome in a particularly Latin way. Like most sadistic psychotics, he kept his penchant for brutality well hidden until he was sure he had captured the emotions of his victim and had transported her to a location free from outside involvement.

This was on the outskirts of Tijuana, Mexico. Here, in 1974, the 2 immersed themselves in a squalid life of drunkenness and brutality. Judy still had not found a place where she could sleep safely at night free from terror.

14

A drunken Judy Kuhn - who'd just turned 16 - sat at a small table with an equally drunken Pepe Reyes in a ramshackle cabana on the edge of Tijuana. Pepe was struggling to read a local newspaper while also using it as a flyswatter.

"Hey, Babe," said Pepe in ragged English, "do you know your dad is making lawsuit over somebody? It in this old newspaper."

"Yeah, some...television station or...or something." She clawed the sweaty hair from over her eyes.

"Why he sue them?"

"They told people my sister's name when...when they weren't supposed to."

"That dead one you always talk about?" asked Pepe.

"Yeah, Sandy."

"Your daddy try to get a million pesos from them, huh?"

"I guess. But he already has millions of dollars. He...he just wants to teach them a lesson."

"I think it time for us to be married now," Pepe blurted.

"For the money? You already knew he was rich. Why now?"

"Now with that extra money he might want to give to us for wedding present."

"I...I don't think so."

"Why not?"

"I...I just don't think so."

"Yeah? Well, I know what you think! That you too good for me."

Pepe exploded into one of his sudden rages. He struck to his feet, rushed upon Judy, screwed her chair around to face him, then punched her flush in the mouth. The young woman flew backwards and slammed to the floor. Pepe then stood over her, bored the toe of his cowboy boot into her stomach and laughed as the woman swam in semi-consciousness.

"We pack and leave in couple hours," he said. "Be ready by then. I go out and check car now. Then we visit your father."

Judy gradually recovered her senses; in more ways than physically. The shock of the latest punch in the face awakened her to the need to escape this lunatic even at the risk of his extreme rage. She remained on the floor for longer than needed, plotting her flight from the madman while Pepe stuffed their few possessions into a pair of suitcases and threw them into the trunk of a beat up old Chevy.

Judy finally dragged herself back into her chair and sipped on a glass of water.

"Okay," said Pepe, "we ready to leave."

"But we still owe 3 months back rent."

"On this dump? We got better pig pens in Brazil than this. We should get paid to stay here."

He grabbed Judy by the shoulder and dragged her out to the car, shoving her into the passenger seat. Pepe then leapt behind the wheel.

When and how - the words kept swirling through Judy's thoughts. When and how to escape. Her chance came suddenly and simply. After driving for about an hour, Pepe ran out of his last cigarette and pulled into a filling station to buy more. All Judy had to do was switch to the driver's seat and speed away. That was all she had to do. But there was a great weight pressed on her shoulder, keeping her in place. The months of threats and cruelty made her fear doing anything against the will of the sadist and she was penned down. So, she sat frozen in her seat until...

Judy snapped the radio on. "Hey Jude, don't be afraid..." Rang out the lyrics from the Beatles song. Was this the spirit of Sandy come to inspire her again?

Judy tugged herself from her seat. She crawled along the front side of the car to be less visible and then squeezed into the driver's seat. Pepe appeared in the rear view mirror just as Judy plunged down on the gas pedal and lurched away. The savage man pursued her with the tenacity of a mad dog until he wore out and fell panting to the sandy ground. And Judy was on her way toward the American border.

After safely crossing the border, Judy pulled over to an observation point where she parked the car and took a deep breath. Hers was the only vehicle at the lookout point. After regaining composure, she got out and walked to the back of the car, opening the trunk.

Crammed in the trunk were a number of hastily packed suitcases and bags, some belonging to Pepe and some belonging to her. Judy hauled Pepe's bags from the trunk and lined them up on the edge of the hilltop, facing them toward the steep slope. One by one she kicked each of the four bags over the edge and as they tumbled and rolled down the hillside she joyfully watched their contents spill out. It was like getting rid of Pepe himself.

Once this was done, Judy returned to the trunk to rearrange her bags. She noticed that sticking out from one of them was a portfolio of the weaving that she had created at the Great House so long ago. She'd forgotten she had it and didn't even remember packing it. Judy yanked the portfolio from its place and carried it to the passenger seat where she sat and leafed through the pages of her own artistry.

Her weaving was good; very good. Her teachers were the best in this field who'd completed their master's work at the Art Institute of Chicago. "Maybe I should go there, too," thought Judy. "Naw, what a crazy idea."

That crazy idea suddenly didn't seem so crazy a few minutes later when Judy found the $2150 that Pepe had hidden in the car's glove compartment. That would be enough to at least get her started toward her newly discovered goal. Maybe it was possible that a person's life could instantly change for the better just like it could so instantly change for the worse.

As Judy straightened out the contents of the rest of her bags, she came across the coon tails that Sandy had so long ago accepted as gifts from an admirer. They filled Judy with added hope and inspiration for the challenges ahead.

15

The time to do battle before the Supreme Court was near. Lawton Philips had spent the last 2 weeks before the date set for the oral arguments studying in his law offices - supplied with catered food and other needs by Marty Kuhn, his generous benefactor. But even though the lower level superior court and the Georgia Supreme Court had given Marty's side victories, Lawton knew that the upcoming struggle would be different and that the forces against him were formidable.

He would be placing the first amendment right of free speech - guaranteed by the Constitution - against the right to privacy which was a right only in that it was customarily upheld by the courts but was not as yet guaranteed by the Constitution. And this particular

Supreme Court was particularly uncompromising about defending the first amendment.

On the night before the scheduled oral arguments, Marty stopped by to visit his attorney - a short, stocky red-haired man in his late 40's. They had cognac and havanas together and sat in the comfortable client reception area at the front of the office.

"Hey, I saw you on television the other night," said Lawton, "cigar and all." "I sneaked a peak at the evening news with Walter Cronkite and there you were."

"That's how important this case is," Marty noted.

"A great, but short interview. That Cronkite gets all the information in a few minutes. Would've been a great lawyer."

"He wanted to know why I was continuing the fight," said Marty. "I told him it was to try to make sure no other families are put through the same thing that we were. Put an end to this irresponsible journalism."

"Commendable motives."

"Big day tomorrow," Marty said.

"It's always a big day arguing before the high court."

"Must be something like I felt when competing for the world bridge championship in '57. Almost won it. Ended the runner-up."

"It isn't bad to be second best in the whole world at anything," noted Lawton. "But, in my case, the runner-up is always the loser. Well, almost always."

Marty poured his friend a refill. "Almost?"

"There was the case of Time Inc. v. Hill, which was argued by Richard Nixon in 1966. I followed his example of locking himself in his office for 2 weeks in preparation for the Supreme Court argument."

"The same Nixon who resigned this last August?"

"The same one. He used to be a pretty good attorney."

"So, what about the Time - Hill case?" Marty sought.

"Well, it was similar to ours. The aggrieved party claimed invasion of privacy because of the negative way he and his family were portrayed in a fictional re-telling of a tragic story about their being held hostage by a gang of criminals."

"Did Nixon win?"

"Yes, and no."

"How did he manage that?"

"The first oral argument was held on April 27, 1966 and the court decided in favor of Nixon on a 6-3 vote. But the decision was unpublished."

"Meaning it didn't count?" Marty asked.

"Uh, basically. One of the judges - Hugo Black - talked the others into a re-hearing of the case which they did in January 1967. This time, the court went against Nixon 5-4. A pretty rare thing."

"And the subject of the case was similar to ours?"

"Very. Nixon argued partially that the information revealed by *Time-Life* wasn't newsworthy and couldn't be protected by the first amendment. Our subject matter is going to be very similar."

"And we're going to win, right?" Marty showed an uncustomary false bravado.

"You never know how the court will rule."

"Bob Larson said you have experience arguing before the Supreme Court."

"A couple of times. It's always a....a heady thing. This one court - the Burger Court - is a particularly interesting group."

"Oh?" Marty said. "How so?

"Well. I'll start with Justice Douglas. He's a real free-thinking type, not what you'd expect for the Supreme Court."

"In what way?"

"He, uh, wrote a couple of articles for what many people consider a pornographic magazine - The Evergreen Review."

"What were the articles about?"

"Nothing obscene or like that. But a fellow judge tried to have him thrown off the court just for publishing in that magazine."

"Really!"

"Then there's Chief Justice Burger himself," Lawton continued. "He's always with the winning side on any Supreme Court decision."

"Is he that...astute?"

"He cheats," Lawton replied.

"Cheats! How?"

"From what I've heard, he waits for all the other Justices to file their opinions before he files his. Then he sides with the majority."

"What if the others tie 4 to 4?"

Lawton shrugs. "Flips a coin?"

"Great." Marty emits a cloud of smoke. "Justice by coin flip."

"And then there's Byron White. Probably the most athletic justice who's ever sat on the court. He was once a runner-up for the Heissman trophy, chosen the second best college football player of the year."

"Ha," laughed Marty, "I probably put down a few dollars on him at some time."

"I couldn't advise you on how to bet on our upcoming case.

"All you can do is the best you can."

"One way or another - it'll be over soon."

Marty nodded. "I wonder what it'll be like to get back to normal life again. Those regular bridge tournaments. I might even be able to visit my daughter, Judy."

"How is she doing?"

"She seems to be doing well. Applied to the Chicago Art Institute and is studying there right now."

"Good, I'm glad she was able to finally get some kind of stability. Hey, you know, I look forward to seeing some of her creations."

"I'll let you know when she's ready to show something. It'll be Thanksgiving in a couple of weeks. Maybe I'll visit her then. Why don't you join us?"

"Is that an invitation?" asked Lawton.

Marty nodded.

"Maybe we'll have a Supreme Court ruling to add to our thanks," said the other man, raising his glass and clicking it with Marty's as a toast.

16   November 11, 1974 - Supreme Court of the United States Chambers

The setting was austere, imposing, potentially overwhelming. Yet, it was just a medium-sized room dominated by one raised and very long judicial bench. But it was the occupants of those seats behind the bench that endowed it with a force of dignity and moral power. Or so it was back then in 1974.

One by one, the Supreme Court Justices entered the chambers and took their places behind austentatious nameplates, led by the Chief Justice Warren E. Burger. It was a solemn and silent procession, the ancient chamber creaking as each man took his seat. Women were not as yet allowed on the Supreme Court.

At this time, the Supreme Court consisted of: William O. Douglas, William Brennan, Potter Stewart, Byron White, Thurgood Marshall, Harry Blackmun, Lewis Powell, William Rhenquist and Chief Justice Warren E. Burger, each of whom possessed his own unique characteristics and beliefs which added to their views of justice and the world.

Below them and seated at their own less impressive desks were the attorneys who would provide the oral arguments on the pending question. Despite the gravity of most matters that were dealt with by the high court, the protocol of procedure was very casual. Oral arguments were prefaced by a simple remark by one of the Justices, usually the Chief Justice and then proceedings got underway. Each attorney would have 30 minutes in which to present his case, with the petitioner arguing first. (What follows is an accurate and faithful account of the proceedings taken directly from court records of the oral arguments that were exchanged during this hearing. Paraphrasing, however, is liberal) .

Burger: The next hearing will concern 73-938, Cox Broadcasting against Martin Cohn. The plaintiff may begin.

David Bender, who'd argue for the Cable Corp, arose to begin his presentation.

Bender: Mr. Chief Justice, other members of the court, the case before you today is a familiar one to you, first amendment rights versus the right to privacy. It does not involve libel. It does not involve false statements. It concerns a ruling of the Supreme Court of the state of Georgia which we contend is unconstitutional.

Burger (a Justice appointed by Nixon and noted for his severely anti-gay sentiments): Continue, Mr. Bender.

Bender: We claim that the law infringes upon the news industry's ability to report the news by putting a limit on its first amendment rights. And this restraint upon the press and on other forms of news disseminating entities is being randomly inflicted across the country, requiring a substantive ruling by this court that will legally enshrine the news industry's rights in this matter.

Blackmun (also appointed by Nixon and the Justice who most strongly favored Roe v Wade): We are aware of a need for clarity on the guidelines set for the news industry, Mr. attorney and agree there is a necessity for a definitive verdict on this subject. That is why we have expedited this matter before the high court.

Bender: Our immediate problem is the negative effects of the restriction of content imposed on us and other agencies by the Supreme Court of the state of Georgia.

Marshall: (appointed by Lyndon Johnson and the first African American to sit on the high court): What form of diminution of rights does the news industry suffer by these restraints imposed on it, Mr, Bender? And what changes are you seeking?

Bender: The loss of freedoms takes many forms. We hope to have all restrictions on freedom of the press and its first amendment rights eliminated.

White (the former All-American football player nicknamed "Whizzer" and appointed by John Kennedy): I assume you do not mean for these privileges to extend as far as allowing libelous statements to stand?

Bender: No, not at all. What I mean to include in those areas which would be untouchable to censorship would be anything that is considered as newsworthy to the public.

Marshall: How has the ruling of the Supreme Court of Georgia limited reporting on so-called newsworthy items?

Bender: By limiting the type of facts that my client was allowed by Georgia law to publish as newsworthy to the public.

Marshall: I see. And what were these facts that your client was not allowed to present?

Bender: The identity of the victim in the rape/murder case that was the news event being covered. The law did not allow us to release her identity even though the information was legally acquired.

Marshall: And this restriction was because the victim was a female juvenile?

Bender: Yes, but she was identified in the indictment by which the offenders were brought to trial and a copy of the indictment was legally acquired by the t.v. news reporter. For authority on the legality of acquiring information this way, I cite: Mills against Alabama and Citizens for Better Austin against Keefe.

Burger: Yes, but the personal information about the victim that we are considering was illegally presented to the public on the evening newscast by that same t.v. reporter.

Bender: That is precisely the matter that we are contending. The act of preventing that information from being disclosed is an infringement on the first amendment rights of the t.v. reporter and the Broadcasting Corporation. The Georgia law is unconstitutional which should be stricken down. It should not have been illegal to reveal the victim's identity.

Rhenquist (ultimately to become Chief Justice and known for adding 4 golden stripes on the sleeves of his robes to mirror the British Lord chancellor) : What criteria do you use in deciding whether or not this type of information should be released to the public?

Bender: If it's newsworthy or not.

Rhenquist: That reply doesn't enlighten me very much. Newsworthy could mean...anything.

Bender: Well, to be newsworthy, an item must be in the public interest.

Rhenquist: Again - not overly enlightening. What makes an item in the public interest?

Bender: One thing, that it is factual information. That's what people watch the news to learn - factual information.

Douglas (the most liberally radical on the court, having espoused many controversial ideas) : Why was it in the public interest to know the identity of a juvenile, female rape victim, Mr, Bender?

Bender: Because it was factual and the public has a right to know what is happening in its community. And this type of knowledge can be very beneficial to the community at large.

Douglas: Oh? How so?

Bender: In situations like the one we're discussing, the more information the public has, the more witnesses appear to assist law enforcement. This is a proven fact.

Stewart (best known for his quote "I know pornography when I see it, and this is not that" in a high court hearing deciding limits of censorship): But in this specific situation, Mr. Bender, the perpetrators had already been apprehended and faced trial; they weren't roaming the streets at large.

Bender: Yet, there could have been other factors associated with this crime that were as yet undiscovered.

Stewart: Were there?

Bender. No. At least, not yet.

White: So you claim that if something is in the public interest this is what makes the topic newsworthy?

Bender: Basically, yes.

White: Who has the ultimate responsibility for determining if something is or is not in the public interest?

Bender: That authority has generally rested with a newspaper's managing editor or with the station manager of a radio or television station. These people are guided by a strict code of ethics which is closely followed by the journalism profession.

Powell (a staunch defender of big business): Would you recognize any other overseers of what is deemed newsworthy?

Bender: Like other professions - the medical field and the legal field - the professionals working in their fields are the best judges of their affairs. Why should it not be the same with the profession of journalism?

Douglas: And when an item that is considered to be newsworthy encroaches upon an individual's privacy, what safeguard would be provided to protect that individual?

Bender: That is what is at issue here. No specific guarantees are granted for privacy of this type. While the Constitution specific-ally protects free speech and freedom of the press as a guaranteed right, no such provision exists for privacy in this specified form.

Brennan (a determined supporter of the Bill or Rights, but a generally boring personality): Which is meant to imply that the right to privacy holds only a secondary place in comparison?

Bender: Yes, while privacy has been protected on a case by case basis, it is

supported only as an intended benefit of other rights.

Burger: Have you an example?

Bender: Yes, a prime example is the 4th Amendment. It guar-antees against unrestricted search and seizure and privacy is only implied as an effect but not as a specified right.

White: And what remedy are you seeking today in regards to your complaint?

Bender: That the Supreme Court grant to our industry the right to regulate itself like other industries have. Let us determine what is in the public interest which is what makes an item newsworthy.

White: And this includes eradicating the sanction against revealing the identity of a juvenile involved in a criminal case?

Bender: At our discretion. On a case by case basis, but so that the restriction placed on our reporting is placed there by us, not by a burdensome law that verges on censorship.

Burger: Anything else, Mr. Bender?

Bender: We request that you overturn the lower court rulings and in this way declare the Georgia statute and laws like it that prohibits identifying Juvenile crime victims and laws like it to be unconstitutional.

Burger: Thank you, Mr. Bender. Representing the opposing side is Lawton Philips, arguing for the plaintiff Martin Kuhn. Mr. Philips you may proceed.

Philips: Maybe it was time that the Supreme Court considered giving protective standing to the idea of privacy as a right. Maybe my opponent has been approaching this question backwards.

White: How so, Mr. Philips?

Philips: Instead of arguing the secondary status of the idea of privacy as the norm, maybe its status should be raised to equal standing with free speech and freedom of the press.

White: An intriguing thought, go on.

Philips: An idea that others have also proposed. In this vein, I cite: North Dakota Pharmacy, Snyder and Tornillo. And, like my opponent I also cite: Mills v, Alabama but to sustain my argument.

Blackmun: (taking detailed notes of the proceedings) It is noted.

Philips: My opponent suggested that the case at hand doesn't involve libel. With that I very strongly disagree and it is this libelous element that is at the heart of the invasion of privacy that my client and his family suffered.

Stewart: How so?

Philips: The victim of the rape and for which crime the 6 boys were being sentenced was the only one named on the now infamous newscast.

Stewart: Yes, that is so.

Philips: An action which on its own marks the victim as somehow being the cause of her own attack.

Stewart: Can you explain how?

Philips: By the workings of basic human nature and societal expectation. The guilty party is named in a crime. Even though in this case the victim was the one who was attacked she assumed the guilt of it by nature of hers being the only name associated with the crime.

Stewart: I can't say that I fully agree with that observation.

Philips: Not long after the victim's name was broadcast by cable news, protests were raised calling for setting free the "Sandy Springs 6." Why? Because in some people's eyes the perpetrators had become the victims of an unjust ruling. They'd been trapped by the victim somehow.

White: But even if the victim hadn't been named, wouldn't the cry "Free the Sandy Springs 6" still have risen?

Philips: Maybe, but maybe not as directly targeted. But the real point is that this behavior interfered with the privacy of the victim's family and loved ones.

Burger: There were other infringements, were there not?

Philips: Yes. Graffiti on public walls, chanting of students on school buses derisive to the victim. Obscene phone calls.

Powell: But that type of activity can never be fully accounted for.

Philips: I'm not so sure of that. In this case, the victim was singled out for abuse. Singled out by being the only one mentioned on that newscast.

Powell: Again, Mr. Philips, the victim is deceased and the deceased have no rights under the law.

Philips: But what of their estates? What of the survivors? I note an earlier citation of a predecessor of mine - Havemeyer v. Havemeyer where the defendant was ordered by the court to remove the body of her deceased 2nd husband from the family crypt due to the sensibilities of the 1st husband's children and the 1st husband's memory.

Blackmun: While this is interesting, it's leading us far afield from the argument at hand.

Philips: But it is this so-called right of free speech that directly subverts the law by making the victim the villain.

Marshall: How so?

Philips: Again, by singling out the victim alone in reporting on the event, the victim is given the onus of guilt. Why? Well, certainly,if others were at fault they would surely have also been named. And so human nature would translate the situation.

Blackmun: Can the reporters be held liable for the instinct of human nature?

Philips: If they are good reporters and know their audience - yes.

Brennan: These reporters believe that if something will be of interest to this public it is considered newsworthy. Is see no problem there.

Philips: Very well. My opponent argued that anything in the public interest is newsworthy and can be disseminated to the public. But who has the authority to determine what is in the public interest?

Burger: Those who are closest to the source of news.

Philips: And are they infallible? Did not the Chicago Tribune once declare Dewey the victor over Truman?

Burger: The lack of infallibility cannot be a determining factor in this question. Otherwise, no one could be considered a proper judge of what is newsworthy.

Philips: True, but who can be trusted with such a responsibility?

Burger: Once again, Mr. Philips, that responsibility should be granted to those who are closest to the source of the news. If you have other points to make, I suggest you move on to them.

Philips: Very well. We all agree that the first amendment is among the most critical rights to a functioning democracy. But are there limits to free speech?

Marshall: Yes, if the speech in question directly results in violence or harm of one type or another. Like inciting a riot.

Philips: Or making the victim's family the subjects of abuse and obscene phone calls?

White: The one matter of most importance in this entire discussion, however, is that the appellant legally acquired the information that was divulged which revealed the victim's identity. Her name was found on a legal indictment which is a public record.

Philips: But this information was used illegally. It's...it's like a person legally buying a handgun and then committing a crime with it.

White: However, can we deny that person the right to buy that handgun?

Douglas: And, denying someone the right to exercise free speech by revealing information he'd gotten legally, is plainly violating the First Amendment. If this court upheld the rulings of the lower courts, that's what we'd be doing - forsaking the First Amendment.

Philips: Cable news claims that the name of the victim was released because it was in the public interest. Why was it in the public interest? All of the other incidents of the crime had been reported - time, location, and the other items involved. Why was the victim's name necessary to know, especially when the names of the perpetrators were kept secret?

Brennan: For completeness, I would imagine.

Philips: This went beyond completeness; it was illegal at the time to release the victim's name. Shouldn't some discretion have been used?

Brennan: It was a matter for the station manager to determine.

Philips: Very well, how can the news industry be expected to act in the public interest and police itself when it discards its own so-called code of ethics?

Marshall: What do you mean?

Philips: According to the industry's code of ethics, it isn't proper to release the name of a female victim of a crime, particularly a violent crime like rape. Yet, that's exactly what Cable News did in the case before us now.

Marshall: Apparently they felt they had some good reason to override the restriction on this particular ethical consideration.

White: All rules have their exceptions, Mr. Philips.

Philips: Including the First Amendment?

White: If the violation is extreme enough. But that doesn't seem to be the case in this matter before us.

Philips: One of the arguments my opponent made to legitimize releasing the victim's name was that by doing so it drew more attention to the crime and in that way would most likely produce more witnesses for the prosecution. It would help solve the crime.

Blackmun: Yes, that was one of the arguments.

Philips: But statistics prove that such an action will more likely scare off a victim of rape and keep her from reporting the crime in the first place for fear of notoriety.

Blackmun: I believe that this matter could be debated but it isn't a central feature of this hearing. So, please continue in a different direction.

Douglas: Mr. Philips, if any information is divulged, spoken of, and brought out in open court it becomes part of the record and is subject to 1st amendment protections. Also, if this information is contained in any legal documents like the indictment it is also a record of the court and subject to being revealed.

Philips: But what of an innocent victim whose name and reputation will be destroyed by the release of her identity? Should it not be kept secret, almost sacrosanct?

Marshall: No! That's just the danger we're afraid of - censorship. There is no legal method for hiding, keeping secret, censoring any information related to legal proceedings. That is where the Georgia law is in error - trying to create an unnatural form of censorship.

Philips: As of now, the news industry has been allowed to regulate itself as to whether or not an item is in the public interest and as such is newsworthy. And, no matter what that item is, the industry is allowed to disseminate it as news. It is our strong belief that this

should be rectified and a more strenuous set of regulations be placed upon an industry which has severely abused its first amendment right.

With that, Mr. Philips nodded a polite bow to the Justices and concluded his argument.

Burger: Thank you, gentlemen. You have both presented your arguments well. The case is submitted.

And that ended the oral arguments. The justices would then study the matter and each would file an opinion in due time. In this case, due time was very quickly for a Supreme Court ruling, and on March 4, 1975 - only 4 months later - their verdict was delivered.

17

When information came to Lawton about the Supreme Court's decision, he contacted Marty and met with him at his law offices. Cognac was laid out for the two of them as they once again met in the comfortable client reception area, seating themselves in over-stuffed arm chairs.

"I'm a betting man," said Marty, rolling his havana between his lips, "and judging by the expression on your face - we lost."

"I'm afraid you're right."

"The only question now is, by how much?"

"It was 8 to 1 against us."

"At least we weren't skunked," said Marty. "Who was the sole good man?"

"Justice Rhenquist sided with us. But even that's a minor victory."

"Why?"

"He agreed with us only because he said that the Supreme Court didn't even have standing to hear this case. In other words, they shouldn't have even put it on the docket."

"There's nowhere to go from here, is there?"

"No. The only way some form of regulation can be applied to the news industry now is by codified law or by amendment passed by Congress."

"And they won't even pass the Equal Rights Amendment."

"It doesn't seem so."

"What exactly did the court decide in our matter? How do things stand now?"

"The Supreme Court ruled that any legally acquired information can be disseminated as news because to deny the news industry this right will abridge its first amendment guarantee against censorship."

"And this includes revealing the identity of a juvenile female rape victim to the public?"

"Yes, they struck down the Georgia law that made it illegal. Now even that information is free to disseminate."

Marty shook his head. "No matter who it harms."

"I tried every argument available. It just didn't matter to them. The only thing that concerned them was freedom of the press and that the news industry alone was responsible for regulating itself."

Marty drew on his havana and sat back. "All I ever wanted was for my daughter to be treated fairly and with dignity."

"We fought for her as hard as we could. Maybe it's time for it all to...fade away. Sandy will find peace in the forgetfulness of the crowd."

Epilog

One of the most deeply and tragically affected persons by the death of Sandy Kuhn was, of course, her sister, Judy. It was Sandy who tried to protect her in her earlier years while living with her mad mother, Olga, and who had plans to free her little sister from captivity but was prevented from doing so by her own death. If Sandy had lived, how great a difference would she have had on Judy's later life!

Because of her brutal upbringing and the privations forced upon her by her sadistic mother, Judy grew up with low self-esteem and the expectation of misery in her life. This brought about self-destructive tendencies which led her into accepting a series of tragic relationships. And the effects that this had upon Judy reflected off of her own personality and soured the interactions that she had with other people. This, naturally, kept her trapped in whatever dismal life situation she found herself immersed in. Could Sandy have persuaded her little sister from getting involved in these dysfunctional relationships? Sadly, her early death would never let that be known. But based on her earlier positive influences on her sister, Sandy would've probably directed her down a healthier path of greater self esteem.

But Judy was a person of inner strength and because she had to deal with an insane parent she'd developed survival techniques which helped her persevere the cruel treatment of later relationships and to escape them. As of this writing (2022), Judy is still living and has been fortunate to find a husband and partner in life who truly loves and cares for her.

Martin Kuhn, Sandy's father, gave up any further attempts to hold the Cable Company responsible for his dead daughter's vilification by the press and television industry. When the Supreme Court decided not to hold this industry to a higher level of responsibility all avenues for doing so were closed off to him and any other citizen who hoped to do so. As of this writing, the verdict made by the Burger court in 1975 is still the law of the land - the news industry is the sole judge of what to disseminate or not disseminate as factual to the public. Martin Kuhn lived out the rest of his life as a bridge grandmaster, appearing at various tournaments and amassing a large fortune from his winnings, gambling successes and through astute transactions in the stock market. He was a man of great intelligence and had a personality which always commanded attention. He died on April first, 2000 at the age of 76.

Sandy and Judy's mother - identified as Olga - as of this writing is alive and in her 90's, still as hateful and sadistic as she's ever been.

What of the perpetrators of the crime that led to Sandy's death? What became of them? None of them served more than 2 years in prison, one as little as 6 months and a third served no jail time at all. None of them suffered the typical hardships of ex-cons because they came from wealthy families which provided them with guaranteed fiscal and social advantages. At least 2 of the rapists went on to become highly successful in business, leading the good life and enjoying their time on earth, raising their children and grandchildren. Something which Sandy Kuhn had been deprived of.

And what of the victim? She is dead. Her reputation at the time had been ruined by innuendo and false reporting. False reporting! Any true journalist would've looked deeper into the story than those who did the smear job on this innocent victim.

The coroner's report proved that the victim had been sexually innocent prior to the attack which killed her. This is a fact, a fact never reported. Instead, the victim was portrayed as a common slut who picked up a carful of boys on the night of a school party with whom to have an orgy. That is the picture provided to the public by the local journalists of the day. The public responded with obscene telephone calls to the victim's family and filthy graffiti painted on walls throughout the town where her murder occurred!

But what are the facts? The victim made the mistake of drinking too much at a party and sought assistance from fellow classmates.

She needed a ride home. The people she asked for help were class-mates whom she knew. The victim only wanted a ride home. She was not in control of who else was in the car or how many other passengers there were. On the way home she fell unconscious and was summarily attacked by several of her classmates, and died. These are the facts.

The problem is that the law that was passed by the Supreme Court made it acceptable for the news industry to present the false report of the victim's death rather than the true facts of what really happened. They were not required to offer the true version, just the version that was "newsworthy." It's a sad thing that what is de-termined to be "newsworthy" even if it is contradicted by the facts can still be presented as the correct representation of the event. This is a supreme injustice!!

So, where is the justice, one might ask? Obviously not here.

The End